# HEAL MY FRACTIOUS HEART

AMBER LAROCK

*A romantic comedy dedicated to the animal lovers, animal healers, and animal rescuers. You deserve something special.*

Copyright © 2023 by Amber LaRock

All rights reserved.

ISBN 979-8-218-20902-5 (paperback)

ISBN 979-8-218-20903-2 (kindle/ebook)

No part of this publication may be reproduced, distributed, or transmitted in any form or by any means, including photocopying, recording, or other electronic or mechanical methods, without the prior written permission of the publisher, except as permitted by U.S. copyright law.

The story, all names, characters, and incidents portrayed in this production are fictitious. No identification with actual persons (living or deceased), places, buildings, and products is intended or should be inferred.

Cover design by Lorissa Padilla, @lorissapadilladesigns

Copy editing, proofreading, and formatting by Kristen Hamilton at kristensredpen.com, @kristenreadswhat

# CHAPTER ONE

The first thing Lila sees when her alarm sounds are two green eyes staring down at her in disgust. If she didn't have a demanding cat that correlates any sign of life with his upcoming breakfast, this would be a terrifying way to start her day.

Lila might be able to get away with one more snooze attempt before Oliver ends it all with a swift paw to her throat, but she might as well begin the uphill battle that is preparing for her shift at the ER.

Having mastered the art of cramming as much work as possible into the shortest time frame imaginable, why would getting ready for work be any different? A glance at the time shows she has a record forty-five minutes to somehow feed her monster, get ready, and make the twenty minute drive across town. What she didn't account for: the inevitable distraction that is TikTok.

Fifteen minutes of cat videos later, Lila scrambles to feed Oliver, get dressed, make sure she has everything she needs, and get out the door. By the time she makes it into the car, she's only running two minutes behind schedule. Pretty impressive for the limited time she gave herself.

Her 10 a.m. to 10 p.m. shift on Friday has the silver lining of working with Zoey, her work and life bestie, but even Zoey can't eliminate the desperate need for caffeine.

She adds Starbucks to her route, knowing it'll add ten minutes to her commute, but she's learned that it's hard to be mad at the coworker who walks in with a peace offering of caffeine for the whole team. It's her secret 'I'm so sorry I'm late' weapon and it works every time.

As she pulls up to Starbucks, she clicks the work contact on her phone, only to be greeted by her favorite voice. "Thanks for calling Southern Star Animal Hospital; this is Zoey."

"Hey Zoe, I—"

"I had a feeling it was going to be a Starbucks day. Hold on, let me get everyone's order," Zoey says with a pause before shouting. "LILA IS AT STARBUCKS! YOU'VE GOT THIRTY SECONDS TO PUT YOUR ORDERS IN."

Lila can hear her coworkers' responses and she makes a quick mental list: java chip frappuccino with whip cream, a matcha latte with soy milk, an earl gray tea, and a hot americano with no sugar, along with her own order of an iced latte.

With the hot bean water of misery on the order list, she knows exactly which doctor is on shift. A man just as bitter as the coffee he orders—Dr. Hale.

## CHAPTER TWO

As Lila travels that final stretch of road before the hospital creeps into sight, she sends a few desperate pleas into the universe. Please don't be a full parking lot. Please don't be a full parking lot. Plea—

*It's going to be one of those days.*

While holding both her lunch box—containing frozen meals—and her tray of 'I'm sorry I'm late' drinks, Lila manages to twist open the back door and stumble into the ER unscathed.

She's greeted by the sounds of fluid pumps and the howl of an epileptic husky, but even with this chaotic choir in her ear, she's happy to see her favorite coworkers.

Lila would like her presence to be the source of the immediate up-shift in the air, but she's willing to accept the fact that it's the eternal joy that is incoming caffeine. She has a theory that a person's coffee order says everything you need to know about them, and it certainly checks out for her coworkers.

First, there is technician Zoey Adams, her best friend and the owner of the java chip frappuccino with whip cream. Zoey is the added sparkle to any shift, but Lila is lucky enough to have her glitter sprinkled on every surface of her life. She's even sweeter than the coffee milkshake she has in her hand, yet she's bold enough to stick up for herself and those around her. She has unruly curls, every pastel-colored scrub combination you can imagine, and a smile that makes her impossible to ignore. Simply put, Zoey is the star of any show.

Next is technician Tara Beckett, the proud owner of the matcha latte with soy milk. Every clinic needs someone to advocate for vegan-friendly options at the next lunchtime learning meeting, and Tara fills this role with pride. She always comes to work with a bouquet of foster kittens in tow, offering every person on shift an opportunity for kitten cuddles after a hard day. Tara is the kind heart you want caring for your pets when they participate in their annual bank account-draining mishap.

Next up is the technician-turned-practice-manager, Susan Miller, the owner of the earl gray tea. Susan is the one you run to if you need help with anything throughout your shift, and I mean anything. You name it, Susan has seen it at least ten times throughout her 30-year vet med reign. She may have a rough exterior and a no-bullshit policy, but underneath it all, she is the solid ground you need to make it through your shift.

The final beverage on the list is the hot americano with no sugar, and this belongs to none other than Dr. Arthur Hale. Dr. Hale is as Type A as they come, which can be particularly difficult at times since life as an ER vet is anything but predictable. He is always intense, likes things done a specific way, and expects the team to be impossibly perfect, but as much as everyone hates to admit it, he's the vet you want on shift when there's a full hospital and a line of pending patients out the door.

Lila savors the first few sips of her iced latte, knowing a full parking lot often means she won't see her coffee again until it has become a lukewarm caffeinated soup.

She looks up at the task board and smiles. Outpatient

today. Zoey and Tara might grumble about this, but to Lila's surprise, she has grown to love working with pet parents.

She may have gotten into the veterinary field due to her love of animals and distrust of most humans, but the clients are her favorite part of the job. She once believed this career path would equate to less human interaction, which is quite the laugh to her these days, but she now welcomes the revolving door of faces with surprising ease.

Lila can't help but smile when she greets her first patient of the day, a chunky ginger cat named Theodore. With such a distinguished name, it's no surprise that this dapper gentleman is sporting a plaid bow tie around his neck.

"He vomited this morning, but that's not the part that has me worried." says Caroline, Theodore's mom. "He barely ate any of his food, and this dude literally lives for food! He once knocked over a trash can just to suck up the juice in an empty tuna can. He's acting fine otherwise, but I'm afraid something is really wrong if he didn't lick his bowl clean."

"I completely understand your concern. You know your little man best, so I'm glad you brought him in."

Lila thought it was impossible to love ginger cats any more than she already did, but here she is, being proven wrong by an adorable little dude in a bow tie. She can barely catch his heart rate over his car engine purrs, and his diligent biscuit making on the exam room blanket has her heart swelling to twice its size.

Immeasurable cuteness aside, Lila manages to pull it together and get the rest of his vitals. She tells Theodore's mom that Dr. Hale will be in any minute, before walking out the door and into the treatment area.

Zoey is struggling to take the temperature of a chihuahua facing the wrath of his little man syndrome. The poor little guy went after his housemate—a dog four times his size—resulting in a large wound on the side of his small, angry behind.

Lila grabs a blanket and comes to Zoey's aid, but once she

5

tags in, she soon realizes the chihuahua is not the only one facing the repercussions of their actions. She forgot to text Zoey to spill the details of her date last night, so now, Lila is cornered and forced to spill. Sure, the date was boring as hell and undeserving of a proper debriefing, but this is besides the point.

"Soooooo?" Zoey asks.

"So what?"

"Don't even!" Zoey laughs. "How was your night? Was he as cute as he looked in his photos?"

"Eh, it was al—"

Before Lila can finish her sentence, Dr. Hale emerges from behind his nearby computer to snap, "Are you going to gossip about your personal life Lila, or are you going to get your patient checked in?"

Zoey and Lila stand wide-eyed in disbelief, and for the first time in Zoey's life, she's speechless. Everyone knows Dr. Hale can be a dick, but this is a new level. To spare everyone the discomfort her response would bring, Lila forces down her frustration, ignoring his comment altogether. *This is going to be a lovely shift.*

With Dr. Hale's attitude behind her, she forges on with the rest of her shift, unwilling to let him get under her skin.

Theodore's mom agrees to run some blood tests since he's 10 years old and on the chunky side, and thankfully, everything is perfectly normal. Since he only vomited once and still has a bit of an appetite, Dr. Hale suggests a dose of anti-nausea medication and a quick boost of hydration with some fluids under his skin.

"I'm on a tight budget right now, but if he vomits again, I can bring him back for more tests, right?" Caroline asks. "I can always reach out to my parents to see if they can help out. Theodore is their only grandchild, so he's kind of a big deal."

"Of course you can," Lila assures her. "Hopefully it's just an upset stomach that will pass, but if he keeps vomiting, we'll need to rule out a few other complications."

Lila waves goodbye to Theodore as he continues to make biscuits in his crate, and while she would love nothing more than to see his adorable face again, she hopes he doesn't have to come back.

∼

It appears as if the animals of Dallas/Fort Worth have conspired together to be as reckless as possible, because the phones never stopped ringing, and the sick pets kept flooding in. Before she knows it, it's 10:00 p.m., and it is time for Lila to throw in the towel and head home to her own bank-account-draining, mess of a cat.

Lila gathers her things and sends her love to the overnight crew because with the way it looks right now, they're definitely going to need it for the night ahead.

She sits in her car and puts the key in the ignition, but just as she turns the key, she feels her phone buzz in her scrub pocket. Pulling out her phone, she finds a text from the last person she expected.

ARTHUR HALE

> I'm sorry. About everything. Can I please come over?

## CHAPTER THREE

Lila has grown used to feeling like she's not enough in her relationships. Whether it has been another woman, a job opportunity, an exciting new adventure, or something else—you name it, Lila has been left in the dust because of it. That's why it was no surprise to Lila when Arthur would get squeamish at the mere thought of building something real with her. It was all she had ever known.

The two had started texting last year when Arthur realized he forgot to give her his share for the fast food run during a nightmare of a shift. Lila would never find out if this had been a genuine attempt at trying to be a decent human, or if it had just been an excuse to reach out to her.

Lila was initially shocked when the grumpy, albeit painfully handsome vet started treading dangerously close to flirting over text. Intrigue is what initially allowed Lila to reciprocate, but before she knew it, she was diving head-first into familiar waters. Nothing excites Lila more than an emotionally unavailable partner, and Arthur was there to offer that crumb of effort she had grown accustomed to accepting.

Texting soon turned into dinners, and dinners soon led to her staying at his place on their days off. There was a lot wrong with Lila and Arthur, but his ease in making her body melt always offered ample distraction from the obvious red flags.

Everything about Arthur is beautiful, from the dark wavy hair on his head to the sturdy and powerful legs that carry him. Unfortunately for Lila, and the hope she had in their love blossoming, Arthur had no intention of Lila being the single admirer of his body.

After eight months of the same excuses and hidden texts with other women, it became clear that this would never turn into the loving relationship that Lila longed for. She had been here so many times before, and she was done trying to convince someone that she was enough.

The tension between the two at work was palpable initially, but they soon got to a place in which their colleagues no longer feared seeing their names scheduled for the same shift.

The outburst at work earlier and the subsequent apology text made Lila's head spin in confusion. The only thing that was more challenging to Lila than establishing boundaries was sticking to them. She felt that familiar pull toward her old pattern of forgiveness, and her fingers were ready to ditch her better judgment and text him back.

*Maybe he knows now that he should have given me more.*

*Maybe my absence in his life made him realize it was time to fight for me.*

*Maybe it will be different this time.*

*Maybe...*

Lila snaps back to reality.

She puts his messages on mute, throws her phone onto the passenger seat, and drives home to the only man that matters: Oliver.

## CHAPTER FOUR

How Lila and Zoey both managed to have Saturdays off is a mystery they had never dared to question, not wanting it to be taken away. They always need a day with minimal human interaction after their Friday shift, so their Saturdays off are typically spent in the bubble of Lila's apartment. Lazy Saturdays are mandatory for Lila's sanity, but she needs it today more than ever.

She hasn't stopped thinking about Arthur since she received his digital apology last night, the one that was about three months too late.

*He's sorry for everything now, only after his ego-driven outburst in front of the entire clinic.*

*Only after three months have gone by without a word outside of work talk.*

*Only after Lila had spent weeks wondering why he put up zero protests to her walking away.*

*He's sorry for everything now?*

Lila's frustration with Arthur is beginning to bubble over, but Zoey is an active volcano, seconds away from shooting lava out of its core.

"FUCK OFF!" Zoey shouts as she reads the irritating text. "He should be sorry for his behavior, but the fact that he thinks his bogus apology is an invitation back into your life—wait...." Zoey pauses. "He didn't come over last night, did he?"

"No!" Lila assures. "I have absolutely no interest in being gaslit after a 12-hour shift, Zoe."

Most of the conversation ending their relationship had been one-sided, but Arthur did make sure to throw in a few unoriginal excuses to make light of her reasoning. Rather than accept responsibility for his wandering eyes—and hands—he tried to blame Lila's growing suspicions of infidelity on her general mistrust of everyone. It was a reasonable effort, but it wasn't going to work this time. Not again.

Nobody had been happier than Zoey when Lila finally decided to end things with Arthur. Lila found out after the relationship ended, over pizza and wine, that Zoey had kept her true feelings to herself when Lila refused to remove her rose-colored glasses, but she always hoped Lila would wake up to it all eventually.

And months later, Lila knows even if it's tempting, Zoey will not let her fall back into her old patterns. Zoey has been there to help Lila pick up the pieces of her messy life for the last five years, and Lila sure did have a knack for getting involved in things that easily shattered.

Most of their Saturdays have the same itinerary—binging their favorite comfort show and eating their weight in pizza—and it has become a treasured part of their weekly routine, but nobody loves a lazy Saturday more than Oliver.

Oliver spends most of his Saturdays hopping from couch to couch based on who's offering the best pats, and whoever's willing to tolerate twelve pounds of fluff digging into their pancreas at once. The only thing worse than Oliver's adorable daggers is the painful biscuit making that is soon to follow.

Lila grabs the nearest blanket to create a buffer between her organs and the twelve-pound monster on her chest, and she notices how even his loud purrs can't drown out the thoughts racing through her mind. "Zoey, why do I always end up right back here? In this same place?"

"Are you referring to our Saturdays, or your messy love life?" Zoey laughs.

Zoey always manages to ground Lila's panic and keep her head from spinning. A life without Zoey's sparkle would be a boring one, but it would also be chaotic as fuck. She's the one everyone goes to for sound advice, so without her, Southern Star would be in shambles.

"I feel like I'm stuck in an endless rerun of a shitty show," Lila says. "Nothing ever changes, and I just sit back and watch it play, over and over."

"I know it feels that way," Zoey says. "But things are changing. You're changing. The old Lila would have never walked away like you did with Arthur. You would have continued to make excuses for him and get off on the mutual toxicity of it all."

"Hey!" Lila huffs.

"I'm sorry, but it's true! It's all you know, Lila. Sometimes I think you may even seek it out."

Lila lets Zoey's words sink in, and she has to admit, she isn't wrong. Lila can't recall a single healthy relationship from her past.

Most of her partners were carbon copies of each other emotionally, and as much as Lila would like to give herself credit, she isn't so innocent herself. She always runs toward those who will never love her back, or at least not in the ways that really matter.

"Think about it," Zoey says. "Nothing ever changes, so you know exactly what to expect. You don't have to worry about the commitment or the work a healthy relationship requires because it won't ever get there. And when you do manage to find something good with someone, you push them out of your life as quickly as they entered it."

Right as Zoey says this, Oliver lifts his head from Lila's chest, sending a judgmental glare across the room.

"Sorry Oliver, but I think your mom's a little toxic sometimes," Zoey says with a laugh.

Zoey is right, as she always is.

It's time for Lila to take some accountability and pull herself out of this familiar cycle, no matter how many times it tries to welcome her back.

Just as Lila begins to shake off the "pep talk" with Zoey, their phones buzz with an email notification from Susan.

Hey all! I wanted to remind you that tomorrow is Emory's first day at the hospital. I gave her the tour today and went over our hospital protocols.
She was the lead technician at her previous clinic, so she should be able to jump right in! She just moved here from Seattle, so be sure to show her your best Texas charm!
Thanks!
Susan

## CHAPTER FIVE

Sundays for most people include any number of activities from time spent with family, to running errands, to relaxing at home, but for the employees on shift at Southern Star, it's anything but relaxing. It's the one day a week every other vet clinic in the area is closed, so all of the sick pets in the DFW area show up at their door.

Lila's standard chaotic morning routine matches the chaos that awaits her at work, but she manages to arrive without the need for apology drinks this time. However, she still squeezed in enough time to get a coffee for herself; priorities.

Taking one last deep breath before diving into what she knows will be the never-ending Sunday rush, she turns the handle to walk in, but is thrown off balance when the door unexpectedly opens into her.

"Oh my god, I'm so sorry!" an unknown voice shouts. "I didn't realize you were on the other side of the door!"

Lila catches herself mid-stumble, grateful she didn't hit the pavement. Her coffee cup is on the ground, the caffeine she needed to survive her shift spilled and wasted.

"This is not how I intended to introduce myself to my new colleagues!" The woman in scrubs says nervously. "I'm Emory, by the way."

"Don't worry about it," Lila responds as she processes the reality that is a twelve hour shift without caffeine. Not only is her coffee now splattered across the concrete, but it made a lovely design on her scrub top as it tumbled to the ground.

The two bend down to collect Lila's coffee cup and lid, and the contents that managed to fall out of her purse, and Lila takes this opportunity to inspect the features of the woman crouched in front of her.

She's opposite to Lila in every way.

Where Lila has auburn hair that matches the freckles on her face, Emory has jet black hair that's almost blue in the sunlight. The woman's arms are painted with patchwork tattoos on top of her tan skin, where Lila has one hidden tattoo she got on a drunken night out.

"I didn't get your name," Emory says as Lila realizes she's been staring too long.

"Yes, sorry. I'm Lila."

"Nice to meet you," Emory says with a smile. "And uh, sorry again. I'll see you inside!" Emory waves before continuing the path she was on before the door collision.

Still in a daze from being bulldozed by a beautiful stranger, Lila makes her way into the clinic, only to come face to face with another dizzying roadblock. Arthur is eating in the break room when Lila walks in, giving her no choice but to acknowledge his presence as she puts her bag away.

It's quiet at first, but Arthur breaks the silence with a question she saw coming from a mile away.

"So, I guess you're ignoring me?" Arthur asks in a passive aggressive tone.

Lila rolls her eyes, unwilling to allow her shift to be ruined by his attitude, once again. "I'm not ignoring you," Lila snaps. "I'm happy to talk about anything other than your half-assed and very belated apology."

"How would you know if my apology is half-assed when you're refusing to hear me out?" Arthur snaps.

With her back still to him, she takes a deep breath before

turning around to speak. "What you're refusing to understand is that I'm not interested in an apology. So if you would stop trying to share with me, I'd appreciate it."

Arthur stares at Lila as she says the words, but in a shocking turn of events, he has nothing else to add. Heart fluttering from the feeling of finally putting Arthur in his place, Lila takes this opportunity of stunned silence to exit the break room, making her way out onto the floor to start her shift.

Most of the cages in the treatment area are filled, occupied by a typical Sunday crowd of patients.

As Lila walks around the room and takes note of who's in the hospital, she sees a dog that helped himself to his owner's Tylenol, a blocked cat that's on day two of his hospitalization, a dog that is in the midst of painting his run with diarrhea, and the list goes on.

Lila would love to turn her head away from the canine artist and pretend she didn't see a thing, but this is one of the glorious perks of the job you simply cannot escape.

As Lila is in the middle of stripping the run of the soiled bedding, Zoey sneaks up behind her, clearly eager to spill the information she's been holding onto all morning. "You wouldn't believe the way Arthur has been sulking around all morning," she says. "Even Susan noticed and asked him what crawled up his ass."

Susan has seen her fair share of tantrums and moody outbursts throughout her time as practice manager, so it's rare for her to pay any mind to the sulking that accompanies a bit of clinic drama.

Southern Star has seen Grey's Anatomy level dramatics over the years. Whether it's due to the clinic being its own dating pool or experts butting heads, opinions are always shared and fighting always ensues.

The clinic doorbell rings over the chaos in the treatment area, and Lila makes her way toward the front door to greet whoever made their way inside.

"Lila! I'm so glad you're in today," Caroline huffs as she carries a cage inside. Within the crate is the dapper kitty Lila met just a few days ago, but unfortunately, he's not the upbeat guy he was before. Theodore is curled up in the crate with his chin resting on his paws, barely mustering the energy to lift his head and greet her.

"He didn't vomit at all on Saturday, but he still wasn't acting like himself," Caroline shares. "But then I woke up to the sound of him vomiting this morning—which is the worst sound to wake up to, by the way."

Lila nods her head in agreement. Every cat mom has experienced this trauma at least once.

"But he vomited once more after that. I think something is seriously wrong," Caroline says, on the verge of tears.

Lila opens Theodore's crate and coaxes him out, and though he has seen better days, he still curls up to Lila's chest immediately. While his purrs are not radiating through the room as they did two days ago, there is still the faint hum of a feline engine. And of course, his adorable bow tie is still in place.

"I'm really glad you brought him back. It looks like it may be time to run those tests we talked about last time," Lila says.

"Yes, of course. Do whatever you think is best."

Dr. Hale performs his physical exam and agrees that it's time to take some x-rays and additional blood tests. The conservative route was okay initially, but he explains to Caroline that it's time to get to the bottom of what's going on.

Lila scoops Theodore up and wraps him in a fuzzy blanket, and they make their way to the radiology room across the ER. Whether it's Theodore's sweet nature or his upset stomach, he puts up no objection to his clinic tour. He doesn't even make a fuss as Lila places him on the x-ray table, really solidifying his title as the best patient ever.

Lila falls in love with all of her patients, but something about Theodore has been tugging on her heart strings from the moment she met him. Every animal caregiver will have those special animals that leave a lasting impression, and Theodore is proving to be one of them for Lila.

As she presses the pedal on the x-ray machine to take his films, she finds herself sending another desperate plea into the universe, but this time with Theodore in mind. No animal deserves to be sick, but especially not Theodore.

As the machine beeps and the images pop up on the screen, Lila feels her heart drop into her stomach. Sure, she may not be able to make the call herself, but she has worked in the ER long enough to know when something just isn't right.

"Man," Arthur sighs as he looks over Theodore's films. "Looks like he needs to go to surgery."

Theodore's films are highly suspicious of a foreign body, or at least something that is blocking his intestinal tract. Caroline never mentioned Theodore chewing on or eating anything he shouldn't be, but really, this means nothing in the vet world. It wouldn't be the first time a cat has pulled one over on their parents, leading to an emergency surgery and a hefty vet bill.

"Oh my god. Surgery?" Caroline asks with tears in her eyes. "Are there any other options?"

"We could keep him overnight on IV fluids and take more radiographs in the morning to see if the blockage has moved, but I've seen many foreign bodies that look like this on x-ray, and I think surgery is the best option," Dr. Hale assures Caroline.

By the time Dr. Hale is in the exam room and breaking down the details of Theodore's situation, Caroline's parents arrive at the ER to support their furry grandchild. Caroline wasn't lying when she said he was a big deal in their family.

"Do whatever is needed to make him feel better," Caroline's mom says. "We all love this little guy more than anything."

Lila makes up a plush cage to hold Theodore overnight,

equipped with his favorite fuzzy blankets and a toy his mom brought along from home. She then walks Caroline to the back with Theodore to get him all settled, and she gives Caroline a moment to say goodbye to her favorite guy before he goes into surgery.

Caroline leans in to give Theodore a big hug, and then cups her hands on both sides of his tiny face. "I love you, and I'll see you soon buddy. You're going to be just fine," Caroline sniffs as she lays a kiss on the top of Theodore's head.

~

Lila spends the next ten minutes getting Caroline all checked out up front, and talking her through any worries she has about the procedure.

"He's going to be okay right?" Caroline asks in a quivering voice. "This is something you do all the time, and cats make it through, right?"

"I promise you, he is in good hands," Lila assures. "Dr. Hale will call you the moment he gets out of surgery to give you an update."

"Will you be with him the whole time?" Caroline asks. "I know it may seem silly, but he seems to really love you. He must be so scared and I—" Caroline pauses to catch her tears. "I think having you at his side will help."

"I'll be with him each step of the way," Lila promises. "Don't worry, I've got him."

Lila takes a deep breath to shake off the heartbreak of seeing Caroline's watery eyes, and she makes her way back to the treatment area to get Theodore started on his pre-surgery care.

But just as she turns the corner to greet him, she's stopped in her tracks by the sight of him already out of his cage. Not only is Theodore not where she expected to find him, but he's on one of the treatment tables, in the midst of having his IV catheter placed by Emory.

Lila just promised Caroline she would be at his side each step of the way, and here he is, already facing the first step without her.

"Um, what are you doing?" Lila snaps as she glares at Emory.

"Oh, I'm just getting him all prepped and ready for his stay. He's staying in the hospital right?" Emory says with a confused expression on her face. "Dr. Hale said he's having surgery."

Maybe it's the combination of Lila's protectiveness over Theodore and the mention of Arthur, but she can't stop herself from bubbling over. "I know what care he needs, but why are YOU doing it? I'm his technician," Lila scoffed.

"Okay?" Emory asks in a sarcastic tone. "I saw that you were up front talking to his owner, so I wanted to help out and get him all settled. Is helping your coworkers a problem here?"

"Inserting yourself into someone else's patient care is the problem," Lila snaps.

"Wow, alright. Seems like an odd thing to be upset about, but I guess it's duly noted," Emory bites back.

Lila looks around the room to see that everyone's eyes are locked on them as they argue, forcing her to pull it together and take a step back.

Emory finishes up his catheter and places him back in his cage, and Lila follows after to get him hooked up to his bag of fluids. Lila was planning to drop the issue and move forward, but she looks down at Theodore's catheter, only to see her biggest pet peeve staring back at her.

"Hey Emory," Lila calls out, causing Emory to look up from the medical notes she's currently writing. "If you're going to take it upon yourself to get patients admitted, you should probably do it right. We write the dates on our IV catheters here."

"Lila!" Zoey says from across the room.

The treatment area falls silent, and Emory is visibly stewing at the public criticism Lila threw her way.

The two lock eyes for what feels like forever, but after a few tense moments, Emory smirks at Lila and goes back to her charting.

## CHAPTER SIX

Theodore's surgery might be the most awkward one Lila has assisted in to date. Most surgeries do involve a bit of small talk among the doctor and the technician when the procedure allows, but that's certainly not the case for this one.

Lila may not be ignoring Arthur as he previously insinuated, but she's not about to be the first one to break the ice. The room is completely silent aside from the occasional question about Theodore's vitals and the need to turn on the suction hose.

Thankfully for Theodore and Caroline, the surgery wraps up without a hitch. It's a good thing Arthur voted to skip a day of hospitalization and go straight to surgery, because Theodore had a major blockage that consisted of five elastic hair ties. That foreign body was not going anywhere on its own.

When Theodore is out of surgery and beginning to wake up in his cage, Arthur sits down to give Caroline a call and let her know that everything went well.

"Oh my god, I am so relieved!" Caroline exclaims loud enough to hear her voice pouring out of the speaker. The next thing Lila hears is, "So that's where my hair ties kept disappearing to! His stomach!"

Cats really are covert troublemakers.

～

Lila sticks by Theodore's side for the first couple hours of his recovery to make sure he is comfortable. While this is the patient care that Lila loves to provide, it is also a great way to avoid butting heads with Emory again.

She can't stop thinking about how sarcastic Emory's tone was throughout the ordeal, and her irritating smirk that accompanied her comments. Lila is getting heated again just thinking about it, but she also can't help but play back that subtle smile Emory shot her way as she looked up from her notes.

Many professionals in this field are passionate about their opinions, so Lila is no stranger to a bit of conflict. But something about her response found its way underneath Lila's skin. Emory was so cool and collected as she fired back at Lila, without a single pause or wavering.

And then there was that smile! That arrogant smile that screamed 'I could not give a fuck about your problem with me.'

It didn't help that her smirk illuminated the irresistible dimple set in the middle of her right cheek. Or the fact that her hair framed her face perfectly as she tilted her head to look up at Lila.

On one hand, Lila is still pissed, and worried about a future filled with awkward shifts and bickering. As if working with her ex isn't uncomfortable enough. But no matter how anxious she is about the potential for a hostile future ahead with her new coworker, she can't help but feel intrigued at the same time.

Once Lila is sure that Theodore is stable, she makes her way back into the surgical suite to tackle the mess they left behind. Assisting in surgery is one of her favorite parts about being a critical care vet tech, but cleaning up after surgery is an instant buzzkill to the high of surgery.

As Lila begins to pick up the sharp surgical tools left on the top of the surgery pack, Zoey enters the room to help her clean up yet another one of her messes.

"Put down your weapons, I'm just trying to help!" Zoey expresses with her hands up in the air.

Lila rolls her eyes as she lets out a laugh. "Yeah, yeah. Really funny Zoe," Lila responds.

"I'm just trying to be safe! Apparently you get squirrely when people are trying to help you," Zoey says with a laugh.

"Alright! I get it," Lila huffs. "I was kind of a bitch."

"Kind of?" Zoey questions with a chuckle.

Lila takes a moment to look back on her confrontation with Emory earlier, and though Emory was armed and ready with a clap back, Lila was being unreasonable.

Yes, she was just being protective over Theodore and wanting to be at his side throughout each step of his treatment, but it didn't give her the right to go off on anyone that challenged her plan. As Zoey previously said, Lila was being a little toxic.

The two remove any trace of the uncomfortable surgery that held Lila and Arthur captive. Lila's conscience creeps in with each gathered tool, making it clear that she owes Emory an apology.

~

Lila sees Emory heading to the break room at the end of her shift, likely about to pack up her things and close out her first day. Thanks to Lila, Emory's first day did not exemplify that southern charm Susan insisted on showing.

Nonetheless, Lila knows this is the best opportunity to apologize to Emory and hopefully turn their work relationship around. Her heart rate speeds up as she opens the door.

"Hey," Lila says awkwardly as she enters the break room. "Do you have a second?"

"Why, am I inserting myself into something else you've claimed right now?" Emory asks as she pretends to look around the room. "Oh, wait. Is this your locker?"

*There's that infuriating sarcasm once again.*

"Ha ha, I get it. That's actually what I wanted to talk to you about," Lila says as she pushes through her embarrassment. "I wanted to apologize for earlier. I was having a weird day and—" Lila pauses. "I was out of line."

*There's that smirk again. And that dimple. And her perfect hair.*

"Okay," Emory says plainly.

"Okay?" Lila questions.

"Yes. Okay."

The two stare at each other for a second, neither of them backing down, no matter how painfully uncomfortable this is.

"I'm really trying here," Lila says with an exasperated tone.

"Look," Emory breaks the silence with a firm response. "I've been doing this for a while. I know what it's like to work with people that take their bad moods and personal dramas out on their colleagues."

"Hey I don't—" Lila chimes in before she is cut off.

"You're sorry, okay. But I'm not the kind of person that's going to hug and make up after being blatantly disrespected. In front of my colleagues nonetheless." Lila stares in shock as she processes Emory's words. "I'll drop it. Whatever. But you're not going to get the sappy reconciliation that you're looking for," Emory says in a calm and collected tone. "Are we done?"

"Yeah. Uh, sure," Lila stumbles on her words, unable to get anything else out after getting her ass handed to her in the most stern, yet unbothered way possible.

Emory makes her way out of the break room, and Lila is left standing there in shock. She's mortified, yes, but if possible, she's even more intrigued than she was before.

25

## CHAPTER SEVEN

"It will be fine! Stop stressing about it," Zoey reassures Lila.

"Are you kidding me? She hates me. She doesn't want me there Zoe," Lila says defeated.

"That's funny, because I told her you were coming and she didn't have any objections," Zoey says with a smirk.

"Well she's not going to tell my best friend how she really feels," Lila laughs.

"Oh my god, will you just stop? You apologized. She dropped it. Move on," Zoey snaps.

"I think you're leaving out a few key parts, but okay," Lila says with an eye roll.

"Great! Now what are you going to wear? I need some inspiration," Zoey exclaims as she digs into her closet.

Susan planned a 'welcome to Southern Star' get together this evening to help Emory feel more comfortable, but after her encounter with Lila, it's probably more like damage control now. At least for Lila's sake, there will be plenty of alcohol to numb the potential sting of another awkward Emory encounter.

The local barcade seems to be Susan's favorite spot to plan the occasional clinic gathering, as it has been the chosen location for the last two Christmas parties and the rare birthday celebration. The arcade gives you an out when you need to escape your tipsy colleagues, and Lila has a feeling she will need to utilize this escape plan later.

You'd think wearing scrubs most days would inspire Lila to go all out when it's time to be social, but Lila chooses not to stray away from her go-to outfit: ripped jeans and her emotional support Fleetwood Mac tee.

This tee shirt has withstood many phases of Lila's life. It's been there for her through nights spent cramming in college, spring breaks she can't remember, dark periods that adhered her to the couch for months, and her current life phase: having no idea what the fuck is going on but going along for the ride.

The green design on the shirt also does a hell of a job at bringing out the forest green of Lila's eyes, and it serves as a perfect contrast to her copper hair.

"Why am I not surprised?" Zoey laughs as Lila emerges from the bathroom in her favorite outfit.

"Okay, what do you think of this?" Zoey asks as she tries to narrow down her outfit choices.

Lila stands in awe of Zoey's style choices as she always does, knowing that no matter which outfit she goes with, Zoey will own the room.

She's wearing a light purple strapless top that cuts off just above her navel, boyfriend jeans rolled loosely at her ankle, and a pair of short lilac heels that pair perfectly against her skin. She has even applied a touch of glitter to the outer corner of her eyes, showing off that signature Zoey sparkle.

"You look perfect Zoe! Don't change a thing," Lila smiles.

～

The two hop out of their Uber and make their way into the barcade, crossing paths with Tara just as they arrive at the door.

"This is my first night away from the kittens in seven weeks! Can you believe it?" Tara exclaims. She takes her foster mom duties very seriously. "I may go crazy and drink two Red Bulls this evening!"

"Do it, girl. You deserve it!" Lila laughs as they walk toward the table Susan reserved.

Seeing your colleagues all dressed up and out of their scrubs is always a unique experience. In the back of her mind, Lila can't help but wonder what Emory will be wearing.

You can never get the entire team at a single outing since the hospital runs 24/7, but Susan managed to round up a great group of people to welcome Emory to the team.

Lila glances around the table, taking stock of the evening's attendees. Susan is in full blown host mode, sitting alongside Zoey, Tara, and three of the Southern Star vets—one of which is Arthur. Of course.

Arthur hasn't reached out to Lila since she put him in his place in the break room, which ironically, would be the scene of Lila's own reality check just hours later. Thankfully, Lila and Arthur's greeting across the table is entirely cordial, so hopefully this means they have a smooth evening ahead.

"You look nice tonight," Arthur says quietly to Lila as the rest of the group catches up on interesting cases from the past week.

Hoping this is just a simple compliment and not an attempt to sniff out a weakness in Lila's stance, Lila replies, "Thanks, you too."

Just as Arthur opens his mouth to say something else, Zoey calls out across the room. "Emory! Over here!"

As Lila turns her head in the direction Zoey called out to, she feels as if the air has been knocked out of her lungs.

Lila thought Emory looked beautiful as she stood before her days prior in her clinic attire, calling her out on her bullshit, but the way she looks tonight is indescribable. Her long black hair is completely straight, falling to the small of her back where her tank top sits loosely against her skin. Her top is tucked into black jeans that hug her hips with ease, as if every piece of her outfit was made with her body in mind.

"Well, if it's not my favorite person," Emory says with sarcasm as she stands in front of Lila.

Lila wonders how time sped up, and how Emory went from entering the room to now standing directly in front of her. Did her reality-defying entrance cause Lila to black out?

"Hey! Uh, good to see you. I—" Lila says with a shaky voice. "I wasn't sure if you'd want me here."

"Well, I considered backing out. But then I realized I'd miss an opportunity to commit the perfect crime in the laser tag room," Emory says with confidence as Lila stares back at her in confusion. "Dark room. Weapons. Limited witnesses," Emory adds bluntly.

"Oh wow," Lila says.

"I'm just giving you a hard time, Lila," Emory laughs just as Susan is pulling her away to introduce her to the vets she has yet to meet at the table.

Lila was still catching her breath from Emory's grand entrance, but now her heart is practically pounding out of her chest.

"Stop drooling," Zoey says with a wink as she smirks in Lila's direction.

Lila would normally think of something smart to snap back at Zoey, but this time, she simply takes Zoey's advice and tries to pull herself together.

As the evening goes on, everyone takes turns asking Emory questions about her life back in Seattle. She is open to sharing about her previous clinic and some of her career accomplishments over the years, but she seems to clam up a bit when things branch into a more personal territory. Susan seems to have insight on why Emory made the move to Texas, likely due to being close friends with Emory's mom, so she jumps in to change the subject any time Emory's voice begins to waver.

Even with lacking quite a bit of context when it comes to

Emory's decision to pack up and head to Texas, most of the Southern Star team can agree that it takes immense bravery to leave everything you know behind and start a new life.

"Good on you for taking a chance and going for it. Many of us here have thought about jumping out of our comfort zone and going somewhere new, but, you know how it goes," Arthur says with praise for Emory. "Last summer I tried to convince Lila to go with me on a two-week veterinary mission to an elephant sanctuary in Thailand, but she was too afraid to get on the plane. And that was just a quick trip," Arthur adds with a laugh.

Lila glares at Arthur across the table as everyone looks on in discomfort.

"Well! Moral of the story is that we're proud of you, and we're happy to have you here, Emory," Susan cuts in just as Lila is ready to commit her own crime against Arthur in the laser tag room.

After a few rounds of drinks and many games played around the arcade, everyone is ready to call it a night and head home. Lila spent the night taking out her Arthur-related frustrations on every target focused game she could find, while Zoey and Emory landed themselves at the top of the laser tag scoreboard with their brilliant teamwork.

As everyone begins to hug goodbye and set off to their cars, Lila sees Emory walking towards her. Lila has managed to steer clear of her most of the evening, but now, she's cornered.

"Hey, I wanted to chat before you left," Emory says with a smile as Lila turns to face her fully, trying not to combust. "I've heard that you feel bad about the other day, which of course, you should," she says with a grin. "Buuuuut, I'm willing to move forward if you promise not to yell at me in public again. Or ever, really."

"Yes. Yeah, of course. Thank you," Lila says with a pause as she stumbles over her words. "I hope you had a good night."

"I did. I hope you did too," Emory replies as she hops into her Uber.

Just as Lila turns around to walk toward her own ride, Emory squeezes in one more comment.

"Oh also," Emory says with a smirk. "Dr. Hale doesn't seem like he would be a fun travel partner anyways."

Emory shuts the car door and rides away, and Lila is left standing in that same Emory induced haze she fell victim to just hours prior during her bar entrance. Lila pulls herself out of the fog and turns around, only to find Zoey staring back at her, a ridiculous grin plastered across her face.

## CHAPTER EIGHT

Lila always wonders how her days off manage to fly by so quickly. It feels like it was just yesterday that she was arguing with Emory in the treatment area, and now another week has rolled around.

When she first started working at the ER, the idea of having four days off each week seemed like an incredible perk. She may have signed away most of her weekends and any major holidays when agreeing to the job, but in the beginning, four days off a week had seemed glorious.

It only took a few months for her to realize that these glimmering four days off were not the perk she had imagined, and her life more so resembled the following:

*On scheduled work days, she worked her* ass off for a minimum of 12 hours, but she brought enough energy drinks and snacks to sustain her for a 16 hour day. She struggled to make it home without falling asleep at the wheel, only to have sleep escape her as the residual caffeine pumped through her veins while trying to fall asleep. Factor in an additional hour of sleeplessness if she had a particularly heart wrenching case throughout her shift. Repeat for each scheduled work day.

*On her first and second days off, she entered* into a coma that only her cat's pushy nudge for breakfast could interrupt. In the hours that she's awake, she questions why the hell she keeps putting her body through this. Once she's had the mandatory spiral, she eats something that requires minimal effort before falling into a horizontal state again. However, she is permitted to eat while horizontal if needed.

*On her third day off, she always caught* up on all the shit she had been unable to do the other days because she was either working or too exhausted. The third day typically consisted of grocery shopping, laundry, cleaning the house, and any other tasks that she was dreading but needed to be done. Once the chores were complete, she could entertain the idea of relaxing.

*The fourth day off is the only day that feels like a* true day off. She always spends this however she chooses, while trying to ignore the crushing reality that come tomorrow, she has to repeat this cycle all over again.

Lila worked three 12 hour shifts in a row when she first started working at Southern Star, but when the opportunity to have Saturdays off with Zoey presented itself, she jumped at the chance. It took her a while to adjust to her new Friday, Sunday, Monday schedule, but she found that the recharge day in between was the extra boost she needed to make it through the week intact.

Somewhat rested and ready to tackle the work week ahead, Lila pulls into the hospital parking lot, armed with her standard shift survival tools.

As she's soaking in the last few minutes of zen in her car, she sees Tara struggling to carry in the two heavy cages that hold her foster kittens. Lila could standby and watch the entertaining struggle that is watching Tara figure out how to open the door in the midst of all of this, but she cuts her pre-shift meditation short to give her an extra hand.

"Ugh thank you so much!" Tara says with a heavy sigh. "I'm so tired. The kittens kept me up all night!"

"Being a kitten mom is hard work," Lila says with a laugh.

"You're telling me!" Tara huffs. "Tortellini won't eat unless his bottle is the perfect temperature. Spaghetti screams at me at all hours of the night. And if that wasn't enough, I caught the new kittens suckling on each other! When will it stop?"

"Sounds like a nightmare," Lila says.

"It was. I had to make them tiny sock sweaters to protect their bodies from the suckling. All at 3 in the morning!" Tara says as she opens the ER door with her free hand.

"I'm telling you. This will be my last litter of foster kittens. I promise!" Tara exclaims.

"Yeah, we've heard that before!" Lila laughs.

"What have we heard before?" Zoey asks as Lila and Tara enter the treatment area mid-conversation.

"Tara says these are her last foster kittens," Lila says in a sarcastic tone.

Multiple responses erupt throughout the clinic, but the collective feedback is a resounding "not a chance".

Lila takes a moment to look around the treatment area to see what patients are in the hospital, and to gather an idea of how challenging the shift ahead may be.

As she glances around the room, she suddenly locks eyes with Emory, who appears to be watching Lila as she's talking to a pet parent on the phone. Emory immediately averts her eyes and goes back to her conversation, most of which sounds like she's reassuring a frantic pet parent on the other end.

"Don't worry, just focus on driving safely. I'll be waiting for you when you arrive," Emory says. "I know, we'll take care of her as soon as you get here."

As Emory hangs up the phone, she begins collecting her medical supplies as she calls out to the rest of the team. "There's a non-responsive 3-month-old puppy that should be here any minute. Her mom says she has had diarrhea and vomiting for the last 48 hours, and now she just collapsed."

Like Emory, Lila has parvo in mind. She watches Emory put on her protective gear after gathering everything needed to help the puppy upon arrival. With a hospital full of patients and knowing more will come in throughout the puppy's time here, no one can risk contaminating their scrubs and exposing more pets than just the puppy.

The front doorbell rings and a woman rushes through the door, holding her unconscious puppy in her arms. Emory begins to run through the treatment area and toward reception, but she manages to shove a gown at Lila's chest as she runs past her.

There's no time to question Emory's nudge to help her run the potential code, so Lila quickly gowns up and makes sure she's ready to jump into action. Dr. Hale must have heard Emory's announcement across the clinic, as he emerges from the office the moment the doorbell rings.

Emory is back in the treatment area with the puppy in her arms within seconds, and it doesn't look good. "3-month-old female Yorkie with vomiting and diarrhea for two days," Lila calls out to everyone helping. "Mom says she didn't eat her breakfast this morning, and she has only had one set of her puppy vaccines so far."

"Did you get a CPR code?" Dr. Hale asks sharply as Emory sets the puppy down on the treatment table.

"Yes, they approved CPR and want us to do everything possible," Emory responds as she begins to prep the puppy's arm to place an IV catheter.

"She's alive, but her heart rate is slowed and she has weak pulses. I'm going to start warming her," Lila says as she collects a warming unit to wrap around the cold puppy.

As if she could do this in her sleep, Emory has the IV catheter placed and has collected a small blood sample within moments of the puppy being on the table.

"Okay, get me a blood glucose once you—" Dr. Hale begins to state, but is quickly interrupted.

"Got it! It says 'Low'," Emory says, meaning the puppy's blood sugar level is too low to register on the glucometer.

As Lila walks to and from the refrigerator to grab a parvo test, Dr. Hale draws up a syringe of dextrose to help boost the puppy's blood sugar. On her way back to the table, he hands her the dextrose to administer and gives her instructions on the puppy's IV fluid rate.

"I'm going to go speak with the owners up front and let them know what we've done so far. If the parvo test comes back positive while I'm up there or anything else changes, come let me know," Dr. Hale says.

~

"Anything yet?" Emory asks from the other side of the treatment table, as they wait for the test results.

Lila glances over at the unfinished test, and responds, "Nope, it's still cooking."

"Hopefully she just has a heavy parasite burden or something. It wouldn't be the first time," Emory says in a hopeful tone.

"Yeah, maybe," Lila says with a shrug.

The two continue to monitor the puppy in silence, unsure if it's their dedication to the job or the residual tension lingering between the two.

As if the silence wasn't painful enough, Emory pulls a Sharpie from her scrub pocket and begins to write the date on the puppy's IV catheter. Just as the Sharpie hits the tape, Emory looks up at Lila with a grin.

*God this is awful.*

"Anyways...," Lila says in an effort to bring an end to the awkward moment. She hoped something would come to her if she opened her mouth, but it became abundantly clear how unprepared she was for the feeling that accompanies Emory's hazel eyes staring back at her.

"Um," Lila continues to stammer. "How are you liking Dallas? Are you getting all settled in?" It's a conversation starter as generic as they come, but Lila is desperate.

"It's alright so far. It's different, but I'm telling myself that change can be a good thing," Emory answers.

"Yeah, definitely," Lila responds.

"Um, is there anything about Dallas that you're enjoying so far? In comparison to Seattle, I mean," Lila asks as she scrambles for ways to keep the conversation going so they don't have to sit in awkward silence.

"Well, the people are great. Warm welcomes all around," Emory says with a laugh.

Just as Lila smiles and nods her head in sarcastic defeat, she glances down at the parvo test to see if anything has changed. There's an extra dot on the test, meaning the poor pup is indeed positive for parvo.

Lila grabs the test and holds it up for Emory to see, and they both share a sympathetic look.

As the two look down at the puppy with sad realization, the puppy begins to lift her head. She doesn't have enough energy to sit up just yet, so she quirks her head around slightly and begins to take in the room around her.

Lila has always thought about how scary it must be for pets to have your last memories at home with their parents, only to wake up suddenly in a hospital with strange faces all around you. Soothing her scared patients is a part of the job that Lila holds most dear, and behind the actual medicine, it's her main priority.

Just as Lila is about to start talking to the disoriented puppy to let her know she isn't alone, Emory begins to soothe the puppy with reassuring pets, telling her that it's all going to be okay. "Hey, hey, it's going to be alright. We're here with you. It's okay," Emory repeats softly.

The way Emory speaks to the scared puppy brings a warm smile to Lila's face, only to disappear immediately once she realizes she is sporting a ridiculous grin.

Just as the puppy begins to come to, Arthur walks back into the room after speaking with the owners. "So, this is Phoebe. Her parents started taking her to the dog park in their apartment complex a couple weeks ago. They didn't realize that she needed all three of her parvo vaccines to be fully protected. So—" Arthur stops mid sentence as Lila holds up the positive parvo test.

"Well, there you go," Arthur says with a nod. "Is she responding to the dextrose and the warming?"

"Yes, she just started lifting her head again. And her temperature is working its way back up into normal territory," Emory shares.

"Okay, great. I'll start working on an estimate for hospitalization then," Arthur says as he walks back to his office. "Stay with her and keep monitoring."

"Well Phoebe, it looks like you're staying with us," Emory says as the tiny puppy rests her face in Emory's palm. It takes Lila a moment to realize that 'us' could mean the two of them or the hospital in general, and she isn't entirely sure which one she prefers more.

~

Twenty minutes have passed since Phoebe first arrived at Southern Star, and she is now laying on her stomach with her head upright, glancing around the room. She is still a bit disorientated and has let out a few tiny howls of confusion, but she manages to wag her little tail each time Emory leans down to calm her. "Okay little one. You're going to have to make a speedy recovery now. You're too dang cute not to," Emory says lovingly.

Lila discusses the details of Phoebe's stay in the hospital with her owners while the tiny pup is coming to, and they have agreed to let her stay for the weekend and reassess how she's doing on Monday. Lila always shares that while hospitalization is often the only way to get a puppy through when they are this sick, there's no way to know if she will come out on the other end. Parvo is such an infuriating illness, especially since it is preventable.

Now that Phoebe is awake and stable, Emory moves the tiny pup to her own private suite in the parvo ward. Just as she is setting Phoebe in the cage and curling a cozy towel around her, her owners come in to say goodbye before they leave.

The parvo ward is small, so Phoebe's dad is left standing at the open door, allowing Lila to hear everything they are saying.

"Oh my gosh. She is awake!" Phoebe's mom says.

"Yes, she was unconscious due to how low her blood sugar was. We gave her some dextrose to boost it, and we'll continue to give her more until she can start taking in some nutrition again," Emory explains reassuringly.

"It's a good thing that she is awake now, right? This means she is going to be okay if she stays here?" Phoebe's dad asks with concern.

"It is good that she responded to the care, but she's not out of the woods yet," Emory continues to explain "If she's improved by the end of the weekend, then I think that will be our sign that she's on the mend. But she's just going to need time."

"Okay, we can give her that," Phoebe's mom says with a sigh. "We feel so guilty. We really thought she was okay since she had her first vaccine."

"It happens. You're not the only pet parents who believed this," Emory says as Phoebe's mom looks at her puppy with tears in her eyes. "All that matters is she's getting the care she needs now. We'll do everything we can."

"Okay. And we can call to check in on her, right?" Phoebe's mom asks.

"Of course, call as often as you'd like," Emory answers with a smile.

Phoebe's parents lean in to pet her one last time before they leave, both with tears sliding down their cheeks. It's clear just how loved she is.

Emory spends the rest of her shift following Phoebe's treatment plan that Dr. Hale created, while also caring for two other parvo puppies that came in throughout the day. It's pretty strange that they even started the shift with an empty parvo ward to begin with, as this time of year, parvo cases are typically rampant. The hot summer sun is finally cooling into a manageable fall warmth, so dog parks and public spaces alike are filled with furry friends spreading their germs.

Lila has had a busy shift herself, but no matter how many tasks came her way, she found herself glancing in Emory's direction at every given opportunity. She saw Emory changing an unending amount of pee pads, replacing soiled bedding on a constant rotation, and aspirating their nasogastric tubes left and right. There wasn't a moment in which she was standing still, and Lila knows she must be exhausted.

"What do you think about inviting Emory out with us tonight?" Zoey asks as she pulls Lila out of her Emory induced trance.

Lila and Zoey always go out on Friday nights after work since they don't have to be back at the ER until Sunday. It's the perfect way to say goodbye to the shit show that is a Friday shift.

"Oh, um. Do you think she'll want to come?" Lila asks hesitantly.

"I don't know. But it looks like she's had a rough day. We can always ask," Zoey says.

Just as Zoey says this, Emory emerges from her parvo cave. Before she has a chance to leave the treatment area, Zoey blurts out, "Hey, Emory!"

Emory turns around with a wondering smile on her face, and Zoey continues with, "Do you want to get a drink with me and Lila tonight? We're just going to a bar called Patty's down the road when we both get off."

"Yeah, sure!" Emory says happily. "I'm off now, so just meet there around 10 when Lila's off then?"

As she says this, Lila wonders how Emory knows the time

she's set to get off work. Sure, maybe she just looked at the schedule, but it was still something to take note of.

"Yeah, I'm about to head home and clean up as well, but we'll meet there around 10!" Zoey says.

"Okay, cool. I'll see you two then," Emory answers as she looks over at Lila with a smile.

How did Zoey convince Lila to spend yet another night with Emory in a bar?

## CHAPTER NINE

Just as Lila pulls up to Patty's, she feels her phone buzzing in her scrub pocket. She sees Zoey's name on her phone screen, and assumes that Zoey is calling to see what's taking her so long.

"Hey! Sorry, I'm just pulling up now," Lila says quickly.

"Don't hate me," Zoey responds, her tone apologetic.

"Why? Wait—are you not here yet?" Lila asks.

"I'm not going to make it after all. I have a massive headache," Zoey whines.

"Girl, you better pop some Tylenol and get your ass here," Lila says sharply. "I'm not going in there by myself!"

"I'm sorry! I really am. I'll join you two another night!" Zoey assures.

"Zoe, you are not bailing on me. I don't even have Emory's number to cancel!" Lila says sternly.

"Don't cancel! Just go inside. Have one drink. It will be over before you know it," Zoey encourages.

The realization sets in, and Lila realizes that she's going to have to manage this one on her own. "I can't believe you're doing this to me," Lila says defeated.

"Text me and let me know how it goes," Zoey says in a chipper tone right before she hangs up.

Lila silently weighs her options before she decides what to do next.

*Maybe she could say she got stuck at work and it was late by the time she got off.*

*Maybe she could say she had car trouble and wasn't able to make the drive.*

*Maybe the thought of Emory's hazel eyes staring back at her sent her into cardiac arrest.*

No matter the excuses that come to her mind, she can't bear the thought of Emory sitting alone at the bar, waiting for the two colleagues that will never show. She can't bail now.

With quite a bit of awkward tension lingering between them, Lila appreciated knowing Zoey was the perfect buffer for their current predicament and the only reason she agreed to invite Emory.

After taking a few seconds to muster up her courage, and texting "*I really hate you right now*" to Zoey, Lila steps out of her car and heads into the bar.

As she walks into Patty's, she's greeted by the usual Friday night crowd. On the makeshift dance floor is the obligatory group of women wearing boas and sashes, and while this can either point to the beginning or ending of a marital commitment, this one appears to be a divorce party.

On the other side of the room three nurses are toasting the end of their own grueling shift, proving that healthcare as a whole requires some form of numbing agent at the end of a long day.

Lila walks past the dancing divorcée and the line of regulars at the bar, but as she moves deeper into the room, a glimmer of long black hair peeks out from behind one of the bar patrons.

Lila walks toward the shimmery hair and the familiar voice coming into focus, and she finally sees Emory, talking to a man in a camo shirt and distressed blue jeans.

"Here's me and my boy Trigger at the park," the man says as he gives Emory a slideshow of his photo library. "Oh, and here's his little brother Ruger! They are the best of buds."

"I see your dogs are big fans of the second amendment," Emory says with a laugh. Just as the man is about to answer, Emory locks eyes with Lila, jumping up out of her seat as if she's desperate to escape the conversation.

"Lila, hey!" Emory says cheerfully. "I saved two seats."

"Perfect. But uh, Zoey won't be coming after all," Lila says nervously. "She just called and said she's not feeling too well."

"Oh, okay. No worries!" Emory says with ease, but Lila swears she sees Emory's body stiffen as she says the words.

Lila scoots out one of the barstools Emory reserved for her, trying her best to play it cool and hide her shaky hands.

"I made the mistake of saying I was a vet tech to the lovely man sitting next to us," Emory explains as she leans into Lila, whispering in her ear. "So of course, he had to show me all the photos of his canine arsenal."

Lila snorts a laugh, and she wonders just how many weapon themed pet names Emory encountered back in Seattle. This is one of the many strange quirks that comes along with living in the south. Just as Lila is about to order a drink, the bartender sets a sparkling drink down in front of her.

"I remembered you were drinking a Tito's and Sprite the other night. I hope that's okay," Emory says as Lila processes the moment. Earlier she acknowledged how aware she was of Lila's work schedule, and now her drink order? *What is happening?*

"I couldn't remember what Zoey was drinking, so...yeah," Emory says with a hint of nervousness in her voice.

"This is great, thank you," Lila musters her response as she tries to hide the fact that her heart is now beating out of her chest.

"How was the last hour at the ER? Anything crazy?" Emory asks just before silence has an opportunity to creep in.

"Nope, nothing noteworthy. Oh, unless you count Tara

spilling a bottle of dewormer down her scrub top. That was pretty exciting," Lila says with a laugh.

"Ah, the veterinary christening," Emory chuckles. "We've all been there."

The two laugh at the thought of the chalky medicine crashing down on Tara's top, only to be followed by 30 seconds of painful silence once the laughter settles. It was inevitable. The two may have shared a few words at the barcade about moving forward, but it feels impossible to break through this wall that was standing proudly between them. Just as Lila is about to muster some courage and speak up, Emory beats her to it.

"Okay, this is still a little weird, isn't it?" Emory chuckles as Lila chokes on her drink.

"Yeah, I was thinking the same thing," Lila says with a laugh as she wipes away the Tito's and Sprite that made its way to her chin as she laughed.

A few more moments pass and Lila knows it's time for her to contribute. "You kind of scare me," Lila admits quietly.

"I scare you?!" Emory asks with a laugh. "You're the one that yelled at me in front of a small audience."

"I know, I know," Lila says as she pauses for a few moments. "Honestly, I think I'm still just a little embarrassed about it. I was out of line."

"Well, yeah," Emory says bluntly. "But we're moving forward. If I'm getting over it, then you have to as well. Deal?" Emory asks as she holds out her hand to shake on the notion.

Lila places her hand in Emory's to solidify the promise as she says, "Okay, deal."

The two shake hands for just a moment, eyes locked on each other as they touch. Lila wonders if she's the only one that feels the sudden rush that comes with Emory's full attention on her, but just as their eye contact intensifies, Emory pulls away.

"So, since we're friends now..." Emory says with a pause.

"Yes?" Lila asks hesitantly.

"Why were you on a warpath that day anyways?" Emory asks. "You said you were having an off day."

Lila barely knows the woman sitting across from her, but still, she can tell that Emory is genuinely interested in what was going through her mind that day. "Well, it's kind of silly honestly," Lila answers dismissively.

"I'm sure it's not," Emory says. "Tell me."

Zoey is the only one that Lila talks to about anything. Work, life, love, all of it. Sharing her feelings with someone new is out of her comfort zone, but she decides to lay down her armor and spill it all. "Well, it wasn't just a bad day, really. It was more like a year of everything boiling over." She pauses to collect her thoughts. "As you may have already noticed from that awkward moment at the barcade, Arthur and I have a past."

Maybe it's the kind eyes staring back at her, or the reassuring smile Emory offers each time Lila pauses, but she shares it all. How they started. How they ended. Everything in between. How hard it was for Lila to walk away, and how hard it's been to remain strong in what's best for her.

"So after I walked away from that conversation with Arthur in the break room, I jumped right into helping Theodore and his mom," Lila continues. "Caroline was so upset, and she was so afraid to leave him. So she asked if I could be with him each step of the way. And of course, we all know that any of us would comfort him as best as we could, but I just wanted to follow through for her."

Lila pauses as she finds her words. "So, when I walked around the corner and you were prepping him for his stay, well, you know."

Emory takes in a big breath as she says, "I get it. I really do."

"Sometimes when we're having a bad day, it feels like the only thing we can do right is care for our patients," Emory acknowledges with a soft smile. "I'm sorry I took away from that, even if it was unintentional."

Something about this moment feels so safe. Lila smiles at Emory, and she feels the wall between them starting to lose its structure, crumbling down brick by brick.

"Well, now that I've laid out the details of my mortifying love life. Let's hear your story. What made you drop everything in Seattle?" Lila asks, changing the subject.

It's clear that this is a painful topic for Emory, as she immediately breaks eye contact and begins to swirl her straw around in her glass. Just as Lila thinks Emory is going to shy away from an answer, she lifts her head again.

"I loved everything about Seattle. My job. My friends. Everything." Emory pauses as her voice begins to waver. "I still can't believe I left. But, I needed to. It was for the best."

Lila takes a moment to imagine what it would be like to drop everything and leave it all behind. To leave Zoey, to leave Southern Star, to leave her cozy apartment. She can't even picture it.

"If you loved it so much, then why did you leave?" Lila asks.

"Everything you described about having an unfaithful partner, I get it. All too well," Emory shares, glancing down at her glass again, avoiding the vulnerable moment between them.

"Do you want to talk about it?" Lila asks, offering the same support that Emory just showed her. Just as Emory opens her mouth to continue, the women from the divorce party crash into the bar around them.

"Heyyyyy! Cutie, can we get five more Jager bombs?" one of the women calls out to the bartender as her arms hang over Emory's chair.

"Jager bombs? People still drink Jager bombs?" Emory mumbles under her breath to Lila. Just as Lila sticks out her tongue and pretends to gag, she locks eyes with the divorcée herself.

"Ladies! Do you want to take a shot with us?" the woman asks enthusiastically.

Lila can't think of anything worse than taking a Jager bomb, but before she has a chance to say no, Emory answers for them.

"Sure! What are we toasting to?" Emory asks as she turns around to face the cheerful woman.

"Fuck men!" the woman yells out in confidence.

"We're toasting to fucking men? All the free shots in the world couldn't get me on board with fucking men," Emory laughs.

Lila almost spits out her drink in response to Emory's objection to the toast. But as she laughs, she also wonders what she means. Is Emory just passionate in her dislike of men, or does she have an actual objection to fucking men? Does this mean she's into women?

Lila's stomach flutters as she considers the thought, but she's snapped out of it when the Jager bomb is placed in front of her.

"Can I suggest an edit to your toast?" Emory asks as she holds up the shot. "I'll get the same point across."

"Of course honey. Lead the way!" the drunk divorcée shouts.

Lila and Emory hold up their shot glasses with the group of women, and Emory begins her toast with pride. "Here's to the women that walked away from men that never deserved them in the first place!"

"Wooh! Yes!" the women shout as they toast their shot glasses and down their Jager bombs. As the women in the divorce party take their shots, Lila and Emory clink their own glasses together, sharing a quick smile before they choke down their shots.

## CHAPTER TEN

Lila and Emory spend the next few hours talking about anything and everything. Their favorite book genres to songs to snacks.

Lila prefers the romance genre, while Emory prefers books with twists that leave her staring at the wall in silence. Emory could never choose just one song to call her favorite, but Lila is passionate that the only correct answer is Fleetwood Mac's classic "Silver Springs." And when it comes to snacks, Lila prefers pickles while Emory loves everything sweet.

After an hour of chatting about the easy stuff, they begin to dive deeper: where and how they grew up, what their parents were like when they were kids and what they're like now, favorite memories, and their childhood pets.

With each memory and thought they share, Lila feels like she's been wrapped in a blanket of comfort and familiarity. The kind of feeling that moves through you when you catch up with an old, treasured friend.

The wall between them has now been demolished and crumbled to a fine dust that lays at their feet, the misjudgments they had for each other sprinkled right alongside it.

They may have begun to peel back each other's bruised

exterior, but the conversation hasn't been successful in unpacking Emory's current timeline: ditching everything in Seattle for a new life in Texas.

Anytime it seems like they are treading closely to Emory baring it all, Emory skillfully redirects the conversation to something lighter.

First it was a sharp turn away from the reason she moved itself, but rather how long she knew Susan. She talked about how Susan has been her mom's best friend for as long as she can remember, and how she's the reason she knew what a vet tech was in the first place.

The next time was much less subtle, as Emory took an abrupt turn away from the topic at hand and dove right back into a conversation about Arthur.

Lila can't help but be curious about her story and what could have possibly led her to make such a drastic change, but now that they appear to be forming a friendship, she figures it's just a conversation for another time as Emory continues to learn to trust her and open up. Because while Lila may not have cracked the Emory code just yet, she knows one thing for certain: she wants to spend more time with her.

"Alright, I'm beat," Emory says as she leans back in her seat. But just as she announces her plans to call it a night, she places her hand on Lila's thigh, making a patting motion on her leg.

It feels platonic at first, but then, the patting motion of Emory's hand comes to a sudden standstill. Lila watches as Emory's thumb begins to graze her leg, her touch so light that she may not have noticed it if she wasn't looking.

The subtle motion sends a tingle up Lila's spine, and a flicker of wanting curiosity comes to life in Lila's chest.

As if Emory can feel the unexpected spark between them as well, she pulls her hand away sharply, drawing it back to the safety of her lap.

Silence fills the air as Lila watches Emory rip herself out of this moment, the current between them now fading to an uncomfortable static.

Lila's heart quietly pleads for Emory to come back, to appease the vestige of curiosity—but the connection is severed.

Lila desperately wants to escape this moment, whatever it is, so she breaks through with her own exit announcement. "Yeah, I'm going to head out as well."

They both gather their things and stand up from their bar stools, and it feels as if Emory is on a mission to get out of Patty's as soon as possible. They make their way through the dance floor and toward the exit, pushing through the wall of the now wasted divorce party.

Lila's cheeks burn at the thought of Emory's hand on her thigh just moments earlier, only to jolt back to reality once the cool parking lot air hits her face.

The cloud of painful silence refuses to release them from its grip, but Lila can't bear the thought of them ending such a good night on such a strange note. "I had a lot of fun tonight," Lila says softly. "I'm sure Zoey will be bummed that she missed out."

"Yeah, I had fun too," Emory agrees.

"You can join us next Friday too," Lila smiles. "Just maybe without the Jager bombs."

"Definitely without the Jager bombs," Emory says with a laugh.

Emory turns and begins to walk towards her car, and Lila can't ignore the feeling of want in her chest. She doesn't know what it is exactly that she wants, but she knows it involves Emory. In a desperate effort to say something, anything, she calls out to her. "Hey! Do you mind telling me how Phoebe is tomorrow?" Lila asks with a pause. "Since I'm not working tomorrow... would you mind keeping me updated on how she's doing?" Lila could have just asked Emory for her number, but after that weird moment inside, this feels like a safer option.

"Yeah, of course," Emory says as she grabs her phone out of her back pocket. "Just add your number."

As Lila puts her number in Emory's phone, she attempts to settle the butterflies buzzing in her stomach at the thought of talking to her tomorrow.

## CHAPTER ELEVEN

"Where did I leave my phone?" Lila asks as she searches around her living room. Blankets and pillows are scattered across the couch in true 'lazy Saturday' fashion, allowing phones to disappear into the blankets as if they were quicksand.

"Did you look in your room? You were just in there," Zoey offers.

"I checked my room already. It has to be in here!" Lila snaps as she digs through the blankets.

"Damn, chill," Zoey says with a laugh. "You were in the kitchen earlier. Did you leave it in there?"

"Here it is!" Lila says with a sigh of relief as she pulls her phone from the blanket's grasp.

While she's relieved to have her phone back in her hand, her relief quickly turns to disappointment when she sees that there are no new texts waiting for her. She opens up her messages just in case her phone has somehow malfunctioned for the first time and withheld her text notifications, but nope, nothing.

Lila's disappointment is obviously plastered across her face, because when she looks up from her phone, Zoey is watching her with concern. "Are you good?" Zoey asks with a slight chuckle. "Why does it seem like you are quietly combusting over there?"

There is no hiding from Zoey. Lila might as well get it over with and come clean, because she's not going to let it go after watching Lila search through her blankets like a maniac. "I may have given Emory my number last night," Lila says coyly.

"Oh my god! You did?!" Zoey says excitedly. "Wait, was this a 'friendly' here's my number? Or was it a 'I've been drooling over you since the second I first laid eyes on you' here's my number?"

"It was more like a 'I have no idea what the fuck is going on, but let's see what happens' here's my number," Lila responds.

"Ahhh, okay," Zoey replies. "But just so we're clear, you have been drooling since the barcade."

"Anyways!" Lila huffs.

Lila wonders if she really has been drooling since they first met, and if so, has Emory noticed? Even through the treatment area smackdown and the uncomfortable conversations to follow, she now wonders if Emory could sense her racing heart and sweaty palms each time.

"Once we got past the initial shock of you not coming to the bar," Lila pauses, "Thanks so much for that by the way."

"Anytime," Zoey says with a sarcastic grin.

Lila rolls her eyes as she begins to say, "Once we finally committed to not hating each other, the conversation was easy," Lila says, pausing. "I could be reading it all wrong, but there was a moment at the end of the night that just felt..." Lila takes a moment to collect her thoughts as she thinks back on those last few moments with Emory at the bar.

"I don't know how to explain it. It just felt different," Lila finally settles on, not knowing how else to explain it..

"Well, maybe it was different," Zoey says kindly. "Don't stress about it. If the night was fun and the conversation was easy, she'll text you. But if she doesn't," Zoey pauses as she shrugs her shoulders, "Maybe it's not the worst thing in the world to avoid another workplace heartache."

Just as Zoey's words begin to resonate, a ding erupts from Lila's phone. Their locked eyes widen, but Zoey offers a reassuring smile that encourages Lila to look down at her phone and see who it is.

On her screen is a message from an unknown number, and it says:

> 214-555-0125
>
> Are you ready for this?

"Are you ready for this?" Lila pauses as she stares at her screen "What does that mean?" Lila asks as she looks to Zoey with confusion.

"Maybe she's trying to be all deep and introspective? I don't know. Is that even her?" Zoey asks.

"Well who else would it be?" Lila says sarcastically.

"Okay, well...play along!" Zoey says with a shrug.

> LILA
>
> Are YOU ready for this?

"Really?" Zoey laughs.

"I don't have anything else to work with, okay!" Lila says.

> 214-555-0125
>
> Oh, I'm living it.

"Okay, is this even Emory?" Lila asks, confused.

Just as she asks the question, a video arrives in the message thread. As Lila clicks play, she sees their parvo patient Phoebe, but she's in a completely different state than she was the night prior. The video shows the tiny pup standing up on all four legs, barking at Emory through the bars on her kennel.

"Oh my god! Look at her!" Lila says with excitement. "She's so bright and alert!"

"Look at that feisty little thing!" Zoey says with a smile as they watch the video again.

Now that Lila knows she is indeed talking to Emory and not a cryptic stranger, she allows herself to dive in.

LILA

> Okay, I definitely was not ready. But OH MY GOD!

LILA

> Please tell her I'm proud of her. It's very important that she knows that.

EMORY

> Done. But I will say, I think the support is going to her head. She is becoming quite the diva.

LILA

> I expect nothing less. What are her demands?

EMORY

> Fresh, warm blankets on rotation.

EMORY

> Her water bowl must be at least 1 foot away from her at all times or she will bury it.

EMORY

> And no more than 30 minutes of no contact, or she will scream. She has proved this more than once.

LILA

> A woman that knows what she wants. I love it.

EMORY

> Not the first time I've let a woman run me ragged.

Lila makes a mental note of another piece of evidence that could point to Emory's interest in women.

**EMORY**
You will never guess who just walked into the ER.

**LILA**
Give me a hint.

**EMORY**
Jager bombs.

**LILA**
Oh my god! No!

**LILA**
The divorcée herself?

**EMORY**
It appears that she has a relation to our Southern Star diva. The grandma I think?

**LILA**
I see where Phoebe gets her strength. How is she alive and well after a night like that?

**EMORY**
Feminine rage is a hell of a stimulant. Seems like she has plenty of it to fuel her fire.

**LILA**
Amen.

"Oh man!" Zoey says as she snaps Lila out of her texting trance. "Susan can't come to the veterinary conference after all."

Susan planned to join Lila, Zoey, and Tara at a veterinary conference in Austin next week, otherwise known as their annual free vacation. Sure, they had to spend most of the time in a lecture hall collecting continuing education hours, but you take what you can get.

"Oh no, why not?" Lila asks, confused as Zoey continues to read something on her phone.

"It looks like she needs to stay behind at the clinic," Zoey says. "She just texted me."

"That's a bum—" Lila says before she's cut off.

"Wait! Emory is coming instead!" Zoey says cheerfully, continuing to read the text.

"Oh!" Lila says with a shocked pause. "She is?"

"Yeah, it looks like Susan just confirmed it with her."

Just texting Emory has made Lila's palms sweat, but the thought of spending two days with her leaves her heart pounding out of her chest.

"Are you okay with that?" Zoey asks in a concerned tone.

"Yeah, of course I am," Lila says in a shaky voice. She's going to have to pull it together if she stands any chance at playing it cool for two whole days.

As if Oliver can sense Lila's nerves from across the room, he jumps down from his cat tree to assume his favorite position on Lila's chest. He immediately gets to work on his biscuit orders, and Lila welcomes the painful distraction that his dagger paws offer. As she pulls Oliver closer to her chest, she gives herself a pep talk that she's too embarrassed to admit out loud that she needs.

*It's just two days. It's just two - DING!*

Lila takes a breath as she reaches down to grab her phone, and she sees that the source of her nerves has texted her back.

EMORY

Save a seat for me on the convoy! Looks like I'm tagging along to Austin.

LILA

Seat saved!

LILA

As long as you're okay with squeezing into the backseat with me and our bags. Tara and Zoey's carsick asses get dibs on the front.

EMORY

I'm looking forward to it ;)

LILA

Me too :)

## CHAPTER TWELVE

Lila always takes the last few minutes in her car before walking into the clinic to savor her coffee and think about the few extra minutes she could have slept. It's only a few quiet minutes, but they always feel essential to have before the chaos she knows will come with her shift.

Just as Lila is about to turn off her car and make her way inside, she sees Arthur burst through the back door and into the parking lot. He's dragging his hand along his face with obvious frustration, but then his hand travels to the center of his chest. His fingers appear to be digging into his scrub top as he breathes deeply, and Lila is immediately taken back to the times spent nursing Arthur through his anxiety.

They didn't occur often, but when they did, Arthur's anxiety attacks were all consuming. Though it's not obvious at face value, Lila learned early on in their relationship that Arthur interprets a lot of his complicated cases as failure. If they don't end with the patient walking out the ER doors with a wagging tail, Arthur would be up at all hours of the night, questioning what else he could have done. As his chest would tighten and his heart would race, Lila always offered him the reassurance he needed to come back.

Lila watches him as she gets out of her car, his hand firmly planted on his chest, she feels pulled between helping and letting him sort it out himself. She knows the logical thing to do would be to just walk into the clinic, but she can't fight the familiar tug that has always sent her running towards him. It's different now, knowing she'll never go back to him romantically, but it feels cruel to walk past him when she knows he's struggling.

Pushing everything else aside, she makes her way across the parking lot and to his side. "Hey," Lila says hesitantly.

"Oh, hey," Arthur answers, looking up with surprise.

"What's going on?" Lila asks, watching Arthur as he moves his hand slowly from his chest to the pocket of his scrubs. Arthur shakes his head silently, as if he doesn't know where to start. "You know you can talk to me," Lila says softly. "What's going on?"

Arthur takes a deep breath as he sits down on the curb beneath him and says, "Phoebe crashed this morning. We weren't able to get her back."

Lila feels her stomach drop as he says the words. It's not the first time she's gotten her hopes up about a patient improving, only for them to take a drastic turn hours later. It's something you get used to when working in the ER, but even so, it still hurts.

"Apparently she became lethargic again late last night, and her abdomen was really painful when they did an exam." Arthur pauses. "Her protein was low on repeat blood tests, so they got approval from her owners to start a plasma transfusion."

Lila watches Arthur as his breath starts to pick up again, so she sets her things down and sits next to him on the curb.

"They said she was stable initially after the transfusion, but she crashed just as I started my shift." Arthur's hand makes its way back up to his chest as he continues. "We did CPR for about 10 minutes, but nothing. We kept trying until we got her owners on the phone, but once I explained how bad it was and how low her chances were, they asked us to stop and let her go."

Lila's mind immediately goes to the memory of Phoebe's parents in the ER just days ago, eyes filled with tears as they said goodbye to their baby.

"Her parents came up soon after to say goodbye to Phoebe in person, but once I got Phoebe in the room with them, they were so angry." Arthur stumbles on his words as he continues.

"Her dad was yelling and saying I should have tried harder. He kept asking why we needed to call him in the middle of the night about a change in treatment, and why we didn't just offer her everything we could from the start. He accused me of being sloppy. Of being negligent."

Arthur grows more uncomfortable with each word, so Lila places her hand on his back as he continues.

"I tried to explain that since she was initially improving, it seemed like we were on the right track. I thought our treatment plan was sufficient." Arthur forces himself to take a deep breath. "But he wouldn't accept that. They left just as angry as they arrived."

"I'm sorry Arthur," Lila says as she rubs his back. "You know this isn't your fault. She was bright and alert yesterday. You were offering her everything you thought she needed."

"I know. I know they are shattered and looking for somewhere to throw the anger, but..." Arthur pauses. "When your treatment protocols are questioned, it's just hard."

"I know, it's not fair," Lila says softly. "They just need someone to blame, but you know how hard you tried."

The two sit silently as Arthur takes in her words. Lila continues to rub his back as his breathing slows, and Arthur turns his face to hers. As if she can sense that Arthur needs to hear it, Lila assures him, "I know how much you care. You're an amazing doctor."

Arthur stares into Lila's eyes, and for a moment, she remembers what it's like to be the one Arthur is focused on.

He reaches his hand up and places it on her cheek, rubbing his thumb against her skin as if he's on autopilot. As if he's picking up right where they left off.

It's so familiar that Lila almost allows herself to forget the last few months, and every painful effort she's made to pull herself out of this cycle.

Just as the moment intensifies, Lila snaps her head to the side, breaking the connection in an instant. The moments that follow are silent, reeling from the jolt of being snapped back to their current timeline.

"This is not why I came over here," Lila huffs. "I just wanted to make sure you were okay."

"I know. I'm—" Arthur says before he's cut off.

"I'm not trying to kick you while you're down, but I mean it Arthur. I came over here as a friend," Lila says sternly.

"Lila, I know. I'm sorry," Arthur says as Lila stares at the ground, unwilling to lock eyes with him again. "I mean it, I'm sorry." She lifts her head and meets his eyes. "Thank you for checking on me."

"Of course," Lila says as she nods her head, before checking the time on her phone, knowing she's now running at least a few minutes late to clock in. "Alright, I'm officially five minutes late for my shift. I'm heading in."

"Alright. See you in there."

∼

"Five minutes late and no apology coffee?" Zoey says with a laugh.

"I know, I know. I'm sorry!" Lila says as she walks into the treatment area. As she's clocking in, she scans the room for Emory, wondering how she's holding up after the incident with Phoebe. Emory was caring for Phoebe most of the weekend, so Lila knows she must be upset.

"Where's Emory?" Lila asks Zoey.

"I think I saw her go into the break room," Zoey offers.

"You still have something to chat about after texting all night?"

Lila laughs and rolls her eyes as she walks away, realizing she feels a tiny flutter in her stomach at the thought of seeing Emory on the other side of the break room door. As she walks in, she sees Emory sitting at the table, but her expression barely changes as she looks up at Lila.

"Hey. I just heard about Phoebe. Are you okay?" Lila asks.

"Yeah, I'm fine," Emory says softly.

"She was such a sassy little girl. Poor thing," Lila replies as she thinks back on the video Emory sent her just yesterday.

"Yeah, it's a shame," Emory says abruptly.

Lila notices that Emory's responses are a bit sharp, but she assumes she is just upset about losing Phoebe. You can't work in an ER without understanding how much that hurts.

"Did you have to talk to her parents when they were here?" Lila asks with concern.

"No, Dr. Hale took over when they arrived," Emory answers as she sits up from the table, preparing to leave the room.

"Hey, are you sure you're okay?" Lila asks one more time.

"Yeah, I'm good. Don't worry about it," Emory says as she walks past Lila and toward the break room door.

"Okay, I just wanted to make sure—" Lila says, but Emory is out of the room before she can even finish her sentence.

*What the hell?*

∼

Lila's Sunday shift proved to be just like any other Sunday, as the phones never stopped ringing and the patients kept coming. Not only did the sick and injured animals of DFW keep her on her toes for 12 hours straight, but she couldn't shake the feeling of something being off with Emory.

It wasn't just the strange interaction in the break room, but the handful of awkward moments that followed throughout her shift.

The first moment was when Lila asked Emory if she could hold her patient while Lila got a blood sample from them. Emory offered a polite "sure" and "you're welcome" after the job was done, but not a word more.

The next was when Lila joined in on a conversation Emory was participating in, where everyone was taking turns in sharing their favorite *Grey's Anatomy* episodes. Lila of course chimed in with her answer—the episode where Jackson storms April's wedding, duh—only to have Emory go silent, withholding the banter that she offered with everyone else's response.

Maybe she was just getting a glimpse into how Emory handles a tough case. Maybe Emory is the type to shut down as she works through it on her own, only to bounce back as usual when she shakes it off. Maybe this is all in her head.

The strange feeling lingers to the very end of Emory's shift, and was present in Emory's goodbye as she walked out the ER doors to head home for the night.

Lila thinks back to the moment at the bar when Emory ran her fingers across Lila's leg, only to pull herself out of the moment with a swift jolt. Was she doing the same thing now? Sure, they were just texting, but it might be too much for Emory.

Lila has allowed herself to get swept up in the Emory allure, but at the end of the day, she hasn't known her long enough to understand her behavior. Just this morning she was feeling embarrassingly giddy about getting to know this mysterious new woman that crashed into her life, but now, she's unsure what to make of it.

One thing she is certain of—she's more nervous than ever for their road trip. Lila's stomach flips at the thought.

## CHAPTER THIRTEEN

"Damn Zoe, are you moving to Austin?" Lila laughs as she loads one of Zoey's three suitcases into the car.

"Hey, we don't all wear the same outfit on repeat," Zoey says with a smirk.

"I'm sorry we're late!" Tara shouts as she and Emory walk up to Zoey's car with their bags in hand. "I was almost to Emory's place when I realized that I forgot to give Susan Tortellini's favorite crinkle ball! I don't think he can go two days without it, so I had to turn around!"

Emory shakes her head and laughs as she shoves her bag into the backseat, creating a luggage wall between the spots where her and Lila will sit. Sure, there's nowhere else to put the bags due to Zoey's wardrobe taking over the entire trunk, but Lila can't help but acknowledge the symbolism here.

"Alright ladies! Ready to hit the road?" Zoey asks with excitement. "We should get there in time to watch the sunset over Pennybacker Bridge! It's just a twenty minute trek to the lookout."

"I thought I broke free of all the hike crazed adventurers when I left Seattle," Emory says with a laugh. "I guess I can never truly escape."

"It's not a hike!" Zoey responds. "It's a brisk elevated walk."

"Don't trust her!" Lila adds. "This is what she does. She lures you in with the promise of an easy trail and a good view, but before you know it, you're three hours into a hike with no end in sight!"

"Whatever! You love our adventures!" Zoey laughs.

"If one can truly enjoy fighting for their life on the side of a mountain," Lila says with sarcasm. "I didn't think I would survive our trip to Colorado together last year. I couldn't wait to get back to sea level!"

"Yeah, I'm thankful I had to miss that trip. I don't think I would have made it out alive," Tara adds.

"Why is hiking always the go-to daytime activity?" Emory asks. "The world needs a low impact option that lies somewhere between getting wasted at a bar and hiking Everest."

"Suck it up you guys!" Zoey says with a laugh. "When we're watching the sunset over the bridge, you're going to thank me for suggesting it!"

Lila and Emory glance over at each other, sharing an eye roll and a sarcastic grin.

"As long as our plans lead us back to the cozy hotel bed at night, I don't care what we do!" Tara says with a deep exhale, speaking as the exhausted cat mom that she is. "I can't even tell you how excited I am for a full night of sleep!"

"Oh, I brought snacks!" Emory shares. "Help yourselves."

Emory pulls a bag of skittles out of her snack pile for herself, and proceeds to hand Lila a snack pack of sliced pickles.

"Do you like this brand?" Emory asks with a soft smile.

"Oh, thank you," Lila answers. "Yes, I love these."

Lila is brought back to the night at the bar when Emory had Lila's go-to drink ordered and waiting for her when—

"Tara, I got you Oreos!" Emory says as she leans forward to hand the bag to Tara. "I remember you mentioned that they are accidentally vegan, minus the palm oil ethicality debate of course."

"Ooohh thank you! Yeah, I do enough for the planet," Tara says with a laugh as she cracks open the sleeve of cookies.

This moment brings Lila to the harsh realization that Emory isn't going out of her way to remember Lila's favorite things. This is something she does, for everyone. It may just be one of the qualities that makes Emory a good friend. These are just friendly gestures.

"Damn, I should have made a point of mentioning my favorite snacks to you!" Zoey says with a laugh.

"Don't worry, I brought plenty of options!"

As they pull out of the parking lot and start their journey, Lila decides she needs a swift change of perspective for her feelings about Emory. This is just a work trip with friends, nothing more.

∼

"Your destination is on the right," breaks through the 90's throwback playlist that Zoey has had on repeat for the last three hours. Zoey believes that no road trip is complete without a Spice Girls tribute, and in her defense, it's kind of true. The only other artists that rank in road trip importance are Britney and Christina, both of which have belted through the car speakers over the last few hours.

Everyone in the car is obviously 'road trip playlist compatible', because each of their voices are sore by the time they reach their hotel. Tara did manage to sleep through the last hour of their concert, as she clearly couldn't wait to dive into her well anticipated hibernation.

"Wake up Tara, we're here!" Zoey says as she pats Tara's leg.

Tara jolts up from her slumber, stretching her arms as she tells everyone how long it's been since she's taken a nap without the kittens in her ear.

"You ready for this?" Lila asks Emory as she peeks over the luggage wall between them, Emory appearing just as unenthusiastic as Lila feels.

"Begrudgingly, yes," Emory says as she bows her head, accepting the reality of Zoey's plans.

The trail leading up to the lookout peeks through the trees, and Lila can already tell it's going to be a steep one. The path is rocky and slick, forcing everyone to look at the ground with each step to avoid a fall. Lila trips over her own feet on flat surfaces, so there's no way she's making it out of this hike unscathed.

"This is nice, right?" Zoey calls out as they start up the trail.

Lila may not be adding hiking to her list of favorite pastimes anytime soon, but she's willing to admit that this is pretty nice. The trees along the path curve over the trail, and it's as if they are in a forested tunnel. An amber hue peeks through the trees as the sun prepares to set, and as Lila glances over to Emory, she sees the copper shine of sun on Emory's dark hair.

The rocks act as a staircase up the trail, so Lila takes her time with each step, pulling her eyes away from the glow surrounding Emory and focusing on the ground. Tara and Zoey are further along the trail like the true overachievers they are, leaving Lila and Emory straggling behind.

It seems like Zoey was telling the truth about the ease of the trail. Within five minutes Lila can already see Zoey and Tara at the top of the path, waving down to them as they settle at the top.

"For once it really was an easy hike!" Lila says to Emory with a laugh. Emory is just ahead of Lila, appearing to be focusing on the steps ahead just as intently as Lila.

"Yeah I can get behind hiking if they were all like—"

Before Emory can finish her sentence, Lila's foot snags on an upturned rock beneath her. It happens so quickly that she can't ground her footing, letting out a yelp as she's sent plummeting forward.

"Are you okay?!" Emory asks with a gasp as she turns around to the sound of Lila hitting the ground.

Lila manages to catch herself before her face makes contact with the ground, but she doesn't make it out completely unscathed. Her knee is now sporting an impressive strawberry, and the sting starts to set in the moment Lila sees the damage.

"I'm okay, I'm okay!" Lila calls out in an attempt to play it cool, trying like hell to fight off the wave of embarrassment that begins to rush over her. Emory is at Lila's side in seconds, crouching over her as she begins to assess the damage.

"I should have known I couldn't talk and walk at the same time," Lila says with a huff.

"Oh no," Emory says with a gentle tone. "Your poor knee." Emory is on the ground with Lila now, her hands placed on either side of Lila's injured leg. "Does it hurt?"

"Not as much as my ego," Lila says with a laugh as she looks at Emory, seeing the look of concern on Emory's face transform into a small grin. As if Emory was waiting for permission to laugh, she finally chuckles along with Lila, placing her hand on Lila's arm as they laugh together.

"Are you two okay?!" Zoey calls out from the top of the trail, her voice high-pitched as it travels down the hill.

Lila yells out, "I'm good!" as she holds a thumbs up gesture in the air, trying to ignore the flush of embarrassment stinging her cheeks.

Emory's hand is still on Lila's arm as their laughter fades, and her hazel eyes find their way to Lila's. Lila is suddenly transported back to the memory of being at Patty's just days earlier, when Emory's hand found a resting place on Lila's thigh. Sure, this moment involves a skinned knee and the sting of humiliation, but as the look in Emory's eyes deepens, everything else seems to fade away. Lila suddenly finds herself mentally thanking that ill-placed rock as she plunges further into the moment, feeling charmed to have this beautiful woman's gaze on hers.

"Do you two need help?" Tara's voice charges into the moment as she calls out to them, likely wondering if they needed to climb back down the hill and come to Lila's aid.

"Go on without me, don't let me hold you back!" Lila says dramatically as she places the back of her hand to her forehead. Emory lets out a laugh as she stands up, brushing the dirt she collected off her pants.

"You're something else," Emory says as she holds her hand out to Lila. "Come on, let's go." Lila takes a deep breath as she places her hand in Emory's, standing up in a smooth motion with Emory's help.

The sunset really is something else. Lila isn't sure if it was worth enduring the public display of her clumsiness, but she can't deny the beauty of this moment. The view overlooks the Pennybacker Bridge and the Colorado River. The sky is painted in stunning hues of orange and pink as the sun sets over the hills, and the steel curves of the bridge appear copper in the glow.

"Thank you for letting me tag along with you to get here, instead of driving myself," Emory says, breaking through the awed silence. "I appreciate how welcoming you've been."

"Of course. We're really glad you came," Lila responds.

"Yeah! We're excited to get to know you!" Zoey says with a smile.

"And we were all new to Southern Star at some point," Tara adds. "It's hard to be the new kid at work."

Emory nods her head with Tara's acknowledgment. "How long have you been at Southern Star, Tara?"

"About two years now!" Tara answers. "I was working at a general practice before, but I was ready for a change. I heard Southern Star was looking for another technician, so I took it as a sign!"

"Oh, so this was your first experience in emergency medicine then?" Emory asks.

"It sure was. I had no idea what I was doing," Tara says with a laugh. "I remember my first day like it was yesterday. It was so intense that I almost didn't come back!"

"Was Lila on your welcoming committee as well?" Emory asks as she turns to Lila, a smirk growing on her face.

"Hey, I take no responsibility for this one!" Lila retorts. "But I'll admit, Tara really did have a traumatizing first day."

"Oh yeah, the patient with the legs, right?" Zoey asks.

"As opposed to the ones without them?" Emory laughs, her eyebrows raising slightly.

"She means the broken legs!" Tara responds. "It was my first day out of training and the first patient I took on my own. I remember it was a slow day for once, and then suddenly, a man came running into the hospital with his chihuahua, screaming at the top of his lungs!"

"Oh shit," Emory exclaims, clearly eager to hear what comes next.

"So of course, I ran up to help, and I'll never forget what I saw," Tara says with a dramatic pause. "The chihuahua was freaking out and flailing around, trying to murder both me and his owner, but both of his front legs were broken!"

Zoey and Lila let out a hiss of disgust as they are transported back to that moment along with Tara.

"I was trying to grab this poor little dude from his owner as he was trying to kill me, all while his front legs were flopping around like wet noodles. It was awful!"

"Yeah, it really was," Lila agrees with a quiet laugh. Lila has had her fair share of traumatizing cases over the years, but she didn't have to deal with any of them on her first solo shift.

"Oh my god," Emory says with a sympathetic chuckle. "That is fucked. What ended up happening with him?"

"Thankfully we got him sedated quickly and he was referred out for surgery, so he's doing great now! Although, he did come back to the ER for an unrelated allergic reaction just a few months ago! And to no one's surprise, he tried to murder me then too," Tara laughs.

"See Emory, your first day could have been worse," Lila says with a laugh as she turns to face Emory.

"Oh yeah, I guess I should consider myself lucky then."

"Well, traumatic first days aside, we really are happy to have you here," Zoey says with a smile. "We needed a bit of new flavor in the group. These gals were getting boring," Zoey adds as she points to Lila and Tara on either side of her.

Lila nudges Zoey's shoulder, and the group shares a comfortable laugh. The sun continues to set over the river, each of them looking on as the colors fade across the sky. Skinned knees and bruised egos aside, this moment is just perfect.

~

After a long day of road tripping and sunset watching, they finally arrive at the hotel. They grab their bags and head into the lobby, with Lila and Zoey making an extra trip back to the car to gather the rest of Zoey's luggage.

"Tara and I are going to share a room. I figured the budding love birds might want their own space," Zoey says as they walk back to the lobby.

Lila hasn't updated Zoey on the current situation with Emory, because well, she doesn't even know if there is anything to tell. She's convinced at this point that the sparks she imagined between them were all in her head, a hallucination brought on by the essence of the Emory allure.

"Oh. Yeah sure, sounds good," Lila says hesitantly.

"Wait, is that okay?" Zoey asks as she suddenly plants her feet and tugs Lila to a stop. "We can switch if you need us to."

"No, no. It's totally fine," Lila assures her.

"Did something happen?" Zoey asks with concern.

"No, no. I don't want them to see us stopped. It's fine, I'll update you later. Come on," Lila says as she moves forward again. Zoey is clearly not happy with the fact that Lila hasn't kept her in the loop with all things Emory, but Lila glances back to see Zoey following her to the lobby begrudgingly.

"Alright, we're all checked in!" Tara says with excitement as Lila and Zoey arrive at the reception desk. "I hope you don't snore, Zoey!"

Tara hands Lila the other room key as she and Zoey walk off, and Lila looks over to Emory as if she's waiting for her objection. She doesn't object, but rather offers Lila a smile as she turns to follow Zoey and Tara. Lila assumes that she missed Emory's brief moment of panic at the thought of them sharing a room when Lila was outside, or maybe, this is yet another one of the scenarios she's dreaming up in her head.

The four of them step into the elevator and ride up to their floor, but they part in opposite directions once the doors set them free.

"Meet in the lobby at 8 tomorrow morning?" Zoey calls out as they walk to their rooms.

"Sounds good!" Lila says back in Zoey's direction.

Lila and Emory walk down the hall in silence, and Lila hopes this isn't a preview for how awkward their room sharing situation will be.

"Man, being your Nightingale in shining armor really wore me out today," Emory laughs.

Lila chuckles as she answers, "I don't recall you offering any strenuous aid."

"Are you kidding?" Emory asks sarcastically. "There's no way you were making it off that mountain alive without my help."

"Oh yeah, the treacherous mountains of Austin." Lila laughs just as she comes to a stop.

"Is this us?" Emory asks.

"Yep, room 302."

Lila taps the room key against the door, and it opens with a soft beep and a click. As Lila struggles to place the room key in the wall slot to turn on the power, she desperately hopes that the light will reveal two separate beds. Lila has accepted the fact that she will be sharing a small space with a woman she can barely look at without her cheeks burning, but sharing a bed will set her over the edge. There's no way—

*It's always one bed. Of course it is.*

Lila feels like she has been plucked from reality and dumped into a cheesy rom-com. Sure, she loves a one bed trope when it's unfolding on paper, but she did not welcome this fictional universe into her real life. There's a tiny couch up against the window, but it looks as hard as a rock. She pauses for a moment as she processes her reality, but she's snapped out of it with Emory's voice.

"Mind if I take this side?" Emory asks as she places her phone on the nightstand. "I may have an irrational fear that involves being kidnapped through a hotel window."

"I mean, that sounds pretty rational to me," Lila responds with a laugh. "Is your hope that you will wake up to the sounds of me being hauled off to my demise?"

"See, I knew you would understand," Emory says with a smirk. "Cool if I hop in the shower?"

"Yeah, no worries. I'm going to unpack," Lila answers.

"Let me guess. You unpack immediately when you get home from a vacation as well?" Emory asks as she raises an eyebrow.

"Yes? Doesn't everyone?" Lila asks with a laugh.

"I shouldn't be so afraid of the window. I have a psychopath right here in the room with me!" Emory says as she walks backwards slowly.

"There's nothing wrong with organization, okay!"

Emory keeps up the act and continues to back into the bathroom slowly, hands raised as if she's in a stick up. She shuts the door slowly once she finally makes it into the bathroom, peering wide-eyed through the opening as she brings the door to a close.

As Lila laughs, she realizes that this is nowhere near as bad as she thought it would be. She's spent the last few days trying to decode Emory's sudden shift in behavior, when there was likely nothing to decode in the first place.

Emory is easy to be around. She's fun. She makes people laugh. She remembers the things people share with her. She comes gallantly to your aid when you slide down a hill.

She seems like a good friend, and just being her friend is enough for Lila.

## CHAPTER FOURTEEN

Lila must have passed out before Emory was out of the shower, because the next thing she knows, she's awake in a dark room. It takes her a second to process the fact that she's conscious, but she soon realizes that the sound of a vibrating phone against the nightstand is what pulled her out of her slumber.

She rolls over to see if her phone is the one responsible for the disruption, but the only thing staring back at her is the time.

*1:13 a.m.*

The vibrating continues, and it's clear now that Emory is the one someone wants to get a hold of. Lila may have been awoken by the incessant buzzing, but Emory is out cold. The light coming from Emory's phone brightens the room just enough to see the side of Emory's face, and there is no sign of impending consciousness.

Lila considers waking Emory up to answer her late night call, but the buzzing comes to a stop. The room darkens again once the notification fades, and Lila closes her eyes as she tries to fall back asleep. Just as she's about to dive back into her dreams, the buzzing starts again.

*Maybe it's an emergency? Should she wake her?*

There are still no signs of life coming from Emory's side of the bed. Lila hates the thought of letting Emory sleep through an emergency call of some kind, so she turns over and tries to wake her.

"Emory," Lila says softly as she pats Emory's arm. Emory is lying on her back with her face pointed to the ceiling, but still, no movement. "Emory," Lila says again, this time pulling on her arm.

"Hmm?" Emory finally mumbles. "What's up?"

"Hey. Wake up. Can you—"

Before Lila can finish her sentence, Emory rolls her body to face hers. She throws the arm Lila was tugging over her waist, sliding her fingers across Lila's skin until they find the small of her back. She moves Lila towards her in a smooth motion, so close that Lila can feel Emory's breath on her skin.

"Oh, um," Lila stammers as she processes what's happening. The room is too dark to see clearly, but she somehow knows that Emory's eyes are on her now. It feels like hummingbirds are whirring in Lila's chest, and all she can think to say is, "wow, um. Hi."

*Hi?*

Is this what she thinks Lila is waking her up for? Is that what Emory thinks she wants? I mean, she does, obviously, but how would Emory know that?

"Is this okay?" Emory asks in a raspy voice.

"Yes! I mean no, that's not—" Lila pauses to collect her words. "Your phone was ringing. That's why I was waking you up."

"Shit," Emory says sharply as she pulls her hand away. "I'm sorry, I thought—"

"No, it's uh…" Lila is officially flustered at this point. "No worries here."

*No worries here?*

Emory sits up quickly to grab her phone, and as she unlocks the screen, Lila can see the sudden change in her expression as the light hits her face. Is that sadness? Anger?

Shock? Lila can't tell exactly, but she can see her body stiffen as she continues to stare at the screen.

"Is everything okay?" Lila asks with concern.

It takes a few seconds for Emory to respond, but she finally does. "Yeah, everything's fine."

Her eyes don't leave the phone screen, and Lila swears she can see Emory moving through a range of emotions with each second that passes. Emory takes a few deep breaths before she finally locks the screen, staring forward as if she is left reeling from whatever, or whoever, it is that just disrupted her world.

Emory finally places her phone back on the nightstand, and she rolls her body away from Lila's to lay on her side. She's facing the other direction now, and the room is suddenly engulfed in a painful silence.

"Are you sure you're okay?" Lila asks hesitantly.

Without turning around, Emory says, "yeah, don't worry. Go back to sleep."

*What just happened?*

Lila can still feel her skin buzzing in the spots that Emory's fingers touched. Emory reached for Lila without a second thought, pulling her in like it's something she's been dying to do. This means it can't all be in Lila's head. Just a few hours ago, Lila was certain that she was imagining every zap of electricity between them. But now?

Lila wishes she was brave enough to say Emory's name again. She would tell her that her soft hold on Lila's back was not only okay, but that she wants to feel her hands on every inch of her body. Want curls in her chest at the thought, but just as much as she wants to say her name again, she can't ignore the sudden shift in the air. This feels like yet another moment where Emory has gone cold.

Lila forces every yearning thought out of her mind, and she finally settles the hum of her racing heart as she drifts to sleep.

## CHAPTER FIFTEEN

"Let's get this day started!" Zoey shouts as they burst through the hotel doors and into the street. The conference is just a couple blocks away from their hotel, so they have plenty of time to get there and hit up the free breakfast before the lectures begin.

Free bagels and coffee may be the reason everyone else is excited to start the day, but Lila is simply eager for a distraction. She cannot wait to be fully immersed in an array of boring lectures, as long as it removes Emory from the forefront of her mind.

"Hi babies! I miss you! Look over here!" Tara says on FaceTime as she makes a series of high pitched noises. Lila can see the blurry outlines of kittens running across the screen, and she's honestly shocked that Tara made it this long without contact.

It's clear to Lila that Emory is pretending as if their brief 1 a.m. embrace never happened, because they damn sure aren't talking about it. Emory appears steadfast in ignoring it altogether, because she was out the door within moments of Lila waking up this morning. She blamed it on the need for immediate caffeine, but who was she fooling?

Now they walk side by side, but this time without a wall

of luggage to block their discomfort.

"Is this it?" Emory asks as her navigation says they've arrived.

"This is the convention center, right?" Lila asks as she looks around, scanning the buildings in sight.

"You guys," Tara says as she manages to hit each of their arms. "Look."

The three of them turn to follow Tara's pointing, and they are faced with a stampede of eager conference attendees turning the corner.

"PENnies," Lila says apprehensively.

"Pennies? Like Abraham Lincoln, pennies?" Emory asks with a laugh.

The group is closing in on them at this point, so they have no choice but to back up and let the cluster of matching t-shirts gain access to the conference doors. A wave of friendly hellos erupts from the group, each of them smiling wider than the last as they walk past them and into the conference center.

"God, they're happy," Zoey says quietly. "Wait, is this what you guys think of me?"

"Yes," Lila says without hesitation, followed by a laugh from Tara.

"Is someone going to tell me what pennies are?" Emory nudges.

"They work with Pet Emergency Network, hence the PENnies. Capital P-E-N," Lila answers.

"I need whatever they're on," Emory says sarcastically.

"I think it's the livable wages and bonuses," Tara chimes in.

"That'll do it," Emory laughs.

Any uncertainty about the conference location has now been resolved, and the four of them make their way inside to get checked in.

Lila has been to a few veterinary conferences in her day, but it's clear that this one is something else. Music is flooding into the hall and shaking the walls, and a flicker of colorful lights dance across the entrance to the main event room. A bright blue carpeted runway sprawls out of the main doors and into the hall, begging them to come inside and see what all the fuss is about.

Stalls of veterinary vendors stretch as far as the eye can see, many of them hosting some form of game or merch wheel to win free swag. There's even a massive game of cornhole being played in the center of the runway, surrounded by cheering vets and vet techs.

*Is this actually going to be fun?*

"Alright, time for breakfast!" Zoey says cheerfully as they take in the room around them.

"Yeah, I might need some more caffeine for this," Emory says with a laugh. Lila understands the need of caffeinated support when faced with a room full of people, and that's not accounting for the added stress of loud music and disco lights.

They follow the arrows to the dining hall, and Zoey takes this opportunity to point out any faces she recognizes.

"Look! That's Dr. Anderson. She does the tiny mic interviews at the dog shelter."

"Oh! That's Joey! He's a zoo technician that shows his day in the life at the zoo hospital!"

"Oh my god!" Tara says as she cuts off Zoey's next intro. "That's Phil the adventure cat! I can't believe he's here!"

Lila and Emory glance over at each other and try not to laugh, knowing full well that Tara will be forcing them to stand in line later for a photo with Phil.

The dining hall is lined with an array of pastries and fruit platters. Lila doesn't even pretend to entertain the end of the table where the fruit lies, and goes directly towards the bagels and chocolate croissants.

"So, how was last night?" Zoey sneaks up behind Lila to ask, obviously knowing she would be near the pastries.

"It was…fine I guess," Lila says reluctantly, almost as if she's asking a question rather than answering one.

Growing tired of her withholding information, Zoey finally snaps, "Enough with the mystery. What's going on?"

"I'm not trying to be mysterious Zoe. I genuinely have no idea what's going on," Lila huffs.

"And why's that?"

"Because," Lila pauses. "I'm still unpacking what happened."

"Something happened?" Zoey says with a grin spreading across her cheek.

"No, no. Not like that. Or, I don't know," Lila says frustrated.

"I have a wild idea. Why don't you just talk to her?"

"That does sound like a healthy way to approach this. But alas, I am me," Lila shrugs.

"Over here!" Tara shouts as Lila and Zoey scan the room for open chairs, quickly seeing that Tara and Emory have managed to snag a table of their own.

"Oooh, great minds I see," Lila says as she sits next to Emory, seeing that her plate is also stacked high with chocolate croissants.

"Why waste time with the fruit when you can get straight to the good stuff?" Emory says in response, sending an infuriating wink in Lila's direction. That subtle wink is all it takes to bring Lila back to the feeling of having Emory's arm wrapped around her waist, fingers tracing up the small of her back.

As if trying to cover up the fact that her mind just teleported back to the bed they shared last night, Lila blurts out, "Alright, which lectures are on the agenda today?"

"I really want to go to the lecture on anesthesia for neonatal and pediatric patients. It looks like it starts in 15 minutes!" Tara says.

"I'm down for that. Then maybe we can go to the one on managing respiratory distress in brachycephalic breeds? Lord knows we'll get to implement those notes," Zoey says with a laugh.

"Let's do it," Emory agrees as she scans the program

schedule. "Oh! There's one on reading ECGs at the end of the day."

"Ugh," Lila huffs. "I'm ashamed to admit how shit I am at reading them."

"Well, here's our chance to change that!" Emory says with a smile.

Ten minutes have passed, so they stack their empty plates and gather their things, ready to conquer their first lecture of the day. Tara and Zoey are waist deep in a conversation about Phil the adventure cat as they make their way across the main hall, so Lila takes this opportunity to follow Zoey's advice.

*Why don't you just talk to her?*

Lila is not skilled in the art of speaking her mind, let alone speaking her mind to the woman who currently has her stomach in knots. Pushing through the flutter in her stomach and the bubble in her throat, Lila musters up the question that's been lingering on her tongue.

"So..." Lila says hesitantly.

"Soooo?" Emory says.

Lila is so close to asking Emory what the fuck is going on between them, but just as swiftly as her bravery set in, it leaves her stranded. Though she's aborting the main mission, she still needs to come up with something, anything.

"So, um," Lila pauses. "You seemed a bit upset last night when you checked your phone."

"Ah, yeah," Emory says quietly.

"Are you sure you're okay?" Lila asks with concern, because though this isn't the main question she had in mind, she still wants to know what's going on inside Emory's head.

"It was just some stuff going on back in Seattle. It's all good," Emory says.

"Alright. Well, you know I'm here if you need to talk," Lila tells her with a smile, simultaneously nudging Emory's shoulder as platonically as she possibly can.

"I know, thank you," Emory answers with a smile.

Lila's fluttering heart has finally calmed from her initial

attempt to ask Emory why she pulled Lila in her arms, before her Seattle interruption took hold of her mind, when—

"I did want to apologize again for last night though," Emory says as her gaze meets Lila's. "It was a mistake. I know you have other stuff going on, and—"

"Other stuff?" Lila interrupts.

"Yeah, I just wanted to say again that I'm sorry."

"We have arrived!" Zoey says theatrically as she opens the door to their first lecture of the day. A few empty chairs are sprinkled throughout the lecture hall, but they make their way to the row of empty seats in the back of the room.

Zoey is already talking to the person in the seat next to her in typical Zoey fashion. It's so often just the two of them, so Lila always forgets just how outgoing her best friend is. Zoey's voice adds to the hum of collective conversations around them, and Lila's mind drifts off to a state of confusion.

What could Emory mean by other stuff? If Emory is referring to a cat that demands every second of Lila's attention, or an all consuming job that she can't mentally clock out of, then sure. Lila has plenty of other stuff going on. But she can't think of anything that would make Emory believe what could have happened last night was a mistake.

"Hello everyone!" a cheerful voice erupts from the front of the room. "My name is Dr. Angela Lopez, and I'm here to teach you all about anesthesia in neonatal and pediatric patients!"

The first slide on the presentation is showing a kitten that appears to be screaming, and the text across the image says "You're still using non-reversible agents in your pediatric patients? Are you kitten me?!"

"So this is a preview of one of the many topics we'll be discussing today," Dr. Lopez says as she points to the screen behind her. "We'll chat about everything from the physiology you should be aware of before approaching their procedure, all the way to the moments they are recovered and heading back home with their families."

Lila can already tell from the enthusiasm in her voice that this lecture will be more than a string of boring words on a white screen.

"If you've attended one of my lectures before, then you know I have a motto when it comes to the care of our young patients." Dr. Lopez pauses. "Does anyone know what that is?"

A few hands dart up throughout the lecture hall, and Dr. Lopez scans the room before she points to someone up front. "Yes?"

"Age is not a disease."

"Exactly!" Dr. Lopez says with a smile. "The age of our patients, whether pediatric or geriatric, should never be an excuse for subpar care. So let's dive into how to best serve our tiny surgical patients!"

∽

Just as Lila suspected from the introduction, it was in fact an interesting lecture. It seemed to set the tone for the rest of the presentations to come, because unlike other conferences in the past, Lila was actually having a good time. The speakers, the vendors, Phil the adventure cat—top tier. All the excitement made the day fly by, and they were finally wrapping up their final lecture.

"Alright everyone, time to pair off! Let's practice some ECG interpretation!" says Dr. Davidson, the cardiologist leading the lecture. As he begins to pass out the practice handouts, Lila hears Emory's voice beside her.

"Alright, let's do this," Emory says as she scoots her chair closer to Lila's, making it clear that she would be the other half of Lila's pair.

Lila hoped she would emerge from this lecture as a waveform reading champion, but as the lecture went on, she was forced to accept that this just isn't her strong suit.

"Are you sure? I'm a lost cause over here," Lila laughs.

"Lucky for you, I happen to be an expert in this field," Emory says confidently.

"Oh really?" Lila laughs.

"Yes. I actually have a formula that helps me interpret even the most complex of arrhythmias," Emory says with a smirk and a head nod.

"Please, share," Lila says as she points to the handout in front of them.

"You'll want to write this down," Emory responds as she taps her pen on Lila's notebook.

Lila plays along and opens her notebook, pretending as if she's ready to jot down whatever genius formula Emory is about to share.

"White on the right, smoke over fire," Emory says confidently.

"Wow," Lila says with a laugh. "That's groundbreaking!"

Lila thinks back to her very first time attaching ECG cables to a patient under anesthesia, fumbling with the chords as she repeated the phrase in her head – *White on the right, smoke over fire*. White cable on the front right forelimb (white rhymes with right), black cable on the left forelimb, and red cable on the left hindlimb. *Don't forget.*

"See. I told you you'd be alright with me on your side," Emory responds.

Lila and Emory laugh, realizing that even with Emory's complex formula in mind, they are probably going to suck at this.

"Lila, Emory!" Zoey says from the table behind them. They turn around to face her, and Zoey is leaned over the table, ready to burst with excitement." A bunch of people are going to some bar called Egos tonight! We should go!"

There's no saying no to Zoey, especially when she's buzzing from the thrill of being social. Lila and Emory look at each other, each of them shrugging their shoulders in a 'why not' motion.

Another night with Emory in a bar.

## CHAPTER SIXTEEN

Lila stares at herself in the mirror, suddenly much more self-conscious about the fact that she's basically wearing the same outfit she always does. Sure, this time she switched up her standard ripped jeans with a pleated green skirt, but her favorite Fleetwood Mac tee is still holding strong.

She runs her fingers through her hair in an upward motion, pleading with it to offer her even a centimeter of volume. She fills the bathroom with a cloud of hairspray to hold her waves in place, only to stop when she sees a text from Zoey flash across her phone screen.

**ZOEY**

We're in the lobby, let's go! :)

Lila is suddenly nervous to open the bathroom door and step out into the hotel room. She thinks back to the night at the barcade when she first saw Emory outside of work, when her reality defying body seemed to alter time. Not only is her heart thumping at the thought of how incredible Emory will look on the other side of that door, but she's feeling something else that has her spooked. It's the most terrifying realization she's had in a long time.

*She wants Emory to want her. To take one look at her, and realize she has to have her.*

Lila takes a deep breath as she turns the doorknob, demanding any sign of nerves to leave her face at once.

As she opens the door to reveal the room, she sees Emory facing the vanity, putting on a pale peach lipstick. She's wearing a white tank top that cuts off halfway down her back, revealing a trail of tattoos that disappear under her shirt. Lila is now convinced that every piece of Emory's wardrobe was made just for her, because her high waisted jeans are just as flattering as the ones she wore at the barcade.

Lila's eyes begin to trail down Emory's body, but she snaps herself out of it, condemning her mind for being no better than a man checking out some woman's ass on the street. Sure, Emory has a great ass, but Lila knows she needs to stop.

"Oh hey!" Emory says, seeing Lila's reflection standing in the bathroom doorway. She turns to face Lila. "You ready?"

Lila swears she sees Emory stiffen for a brief moment as they lock eyes. Emory's eyes make a quick pass over Lila's body, pausing just before she says, "You look good!"

She says it in a way that friends would, as if she's simply complimenting her outfit choice for a night out.

"Thanks. You do too," Lila says back to Emory, unsure of what to make of that brief pause before Emory's feedback. "Ready to go?"

"Yep, let's do it!"

~

"Are you sure it's here? These are just apartments," Tara asks.

"I don't know, but it says we've arrived," Lila says as she spins around slowly, looking for any evidence of a bar.

"Ooh! I think I hear music. This way!" Emory says as she walks deeper into the complex, heading toward the faint sound of bass thumping and voices chattering.

As they turn the corner, the sounds get louder, and a group of people on the other side of the parking lot come into focus. They may not be wearing their matching t-shirts this evening, but there's no denying who they are—the PENnies.

"Wow, they're like a beacon when you're lost, aren't they?" Emory laughs.

"Alright PENnies, lead the way!" Zoey shouts.

They turn to the left and see an underpass where two apartment buildings meet. A red glow illuminates the walkway, and the entrance of the bar comes into focus. It's a gem hidden along the outskirts of the 6th Street chaos, and it's a true dive bar. It reminds Lila of Patty's, and a wave of familiarity comforts her.

As they step further into Ego's and the rest of the bar is revealed, a simultaneous "Oh my god" is released from both Zoey and Emory's lips. While Zoey's tone is pure, unadulterated joy, Emory's is complete horror.

Karaoke. It's a karaoke bar.

Zoey always says that the one thing Patty's is missing is karaoke. This bar not only has it, but there's an actual stage dedicated to their intoxicated performers. It's a good thing Zoey packed her entire wardrobe for this trip, because now Lila is sure that Zoey will actually be moving here after all.

"How many Tito's and Sprites will you need to get up there and show us what you've got?" Emory asks Lila as they lean over the bar, waiting to order their drinks.

"Oh god. I think I'd need to skip the Sprite and just sip on the bottle," Lila laughs.

"Lila, can you get me a cider? I need to put my name on the karaoke list!" Zoey asks in a hurry, as if singing on that stage is her life's mission.

Lila chuckles as she agrees, unable to wrap her mind around the fact that Zoey doesn't need a drop of alcohol to warm her up to the idea of singing in front of strangers.

"Zoey might be my favorite person ever," Emory says with a laugh as she watches Zoey run to the sign up sheet. Zoey is the most important person in Lila's life, so she loves when other people appreciate how bright Zoey shines.

"She's great, isn't she?" Lila says in agreement. A moment later, the bartender takes their drink orders, and a few minutes later they have their drinks in hand.

There's an open table close to the makeshift stage, so they quickly claim it as their own before anyone else can. Zoey is still waiting in line to add her name to the karaoke list, so Lila scans the room in search of Tara. Her eyes find her in the corner of the bar with a soda in hand, making exaggerated faces at her phone screen. Lila smiles as Tara calls out to her kittens through the screen, and Emory turns in her chair to see what has Lila's attention.

Emory is laughing as she turns back to face Lila, and she takes a breath before saying, "I really lucked out with finding the three of you!" A tender smile spreads across Emory's face just as she says it.

"And why's that?" Lila asks, unsure of what she means.

"I could have ended up at a clinic with a bunch of weirdos," Emory says. "I mean, Susan said everyone at Southern Star was nice, but I really had no idea what to expect. I was really nervous about what I could've been walking into."

Lila smiles at the thought of Emory being happy with her current life path, but then she is hit with a flashback of Emory's first day at the ER, Lila sounding off on her across the treatment area.

"Oh god. I'm sure I didn't help to ease your nerves about your future coworkers," Lila says with a wince.

Emory laughs as she says, "Yeah, I won't lie. You had me scared there for a second." Emory pauses. "But Susan told me it was out of character for you, so I was open to giving you a second chance." Emory winks, and that infuriatingly sexy wink makes Lila's head spin.

The wink is almost too much for Lila to bear, but Emory

delivers the final blow when she says, "I'm really glad I gave this a second chance."

Their stare intensifies, and Lila has to change the subject to prevent herself from melting in her chair. She lightens the intensity of the moment with, "on the topic of you being blessed with such amazing new friends, how did your friends in Seattle feel about you moving to Texas?"

Lila can see the expression on Emory's face change, but her immediate response shows her that she's open to having the conversation.

"Things got really complicated, so they understood why I needed to leave," Emory says quietly, looking down at the table.

"Oh," Lila answers as her eyebrows scrunched together. "Complicated how?"

Emory takes a deep breath as she says, "Well, I went through a bad breakup a few months ago. We had the same close circle of friends, so things got really messy. People choosing sides and what not."

"Oh, wow. That must have been awful," Lila says in response, trying to imagine what it would be like to go through a breakup without Zoey, unwavering at her side.

"I never asked anyone to choose sides, of course. But with the way it all went down, there was so much resentment. Our friendships were forever changed."

"God, I'm sorry," Lila says, tempted to reach over and grab Emory's hand that's resting on the table.

"It's okay. I was ready for a new start, and it seems like I got a pretty good one." Emory's dimple is on full display as she smiles, and Lila practically melts. Just moments ago Emory was telling Lila how lucky she felt to be at Southern Star, but now, the one feeling lucky is Lila.

"Guess who's performing a 90's pop classic with yours truly!" Zoey exclaims as she sits down in the chair next to Lila.

"Not me, I hope," Lila answers with a laugh.

"Unfortunately, it is me," Tara says as she bows her head, accepting her fate as she slinks down into her chair.

"How did you let her do this to you Tara?" Lila asks sarcastically. "You should have stayed on the line with your kittens!"

"Ugh I wanted to," Tara responds. "But Susan told me I needed to stop calling and let them all get some sleep. So here we are."

"Please! You two will be begging me to join you on stage by the end of the night," Zoey says as she picks up her cider, flipping her hair with her free hand.

Suddenly, an unmistakable intro erupts from the speakers. If Lila didn't already know this was Zoey's chosen karaoke song based on how many times she played it on the way to Austin, the announcer calling Zoey to the stage cleared up any uncertainty. Zoey pushes out of her chair and runs toward the stage, Tara dragging her feet slowly behind her.

With microphone in hand, Zoey belts out the opening line and then completely owns the first verse of Christina Aguilera's "Genie in a Bottle." She turns to Tara as the song continues.

Lila and Emory send a few "Woohs!" into the air, cheering their friends on with each passing verse. "Genie In A Bottle" is obviously a crowd favorite, because the entire room is singing each word right along with them.

The energy in the bar is immaculate, and just when you think it couldn't get any better, Zoey closes out the song by getting down on her hands and knees, pretending to crawl in the sand like Christina Aguilera in the music video. Tara bends over with laughter at her outrageous co-star, unable to contribute to the last line of the song.

If this is their current reality just fifteen minutes into their bar arrival, Lila can't even begin to imagine what's in store for the rest of the night.

∼

A few hours pass, and Lila is five drinks deep. Emory is tied right alongside Lila, and Zoey is quickly catching up. Tara made the switch from Coke to Red Bull, understanding that she likely has a long night ahead of her.

"I'm going to get another drink. Does anybody want anything?" Emory asks as she stands up from their table.

"Ooh, I'll have another!" Zoey says with a smile.

Lila and Tara both say they are set for now, and Emory heads to the bar to get her and Zoey's next round. Lila finds herself watching Emory as she walks across the room, eyes settling as she leans her body against the bar. Just as she's about to pull her focus away, she sees a man approach Emory.

At first she's not sure if he just happens to be standing there next to Emory, trying to get the bartender's attention just like everyone else. But his intentions are clear when he leans over and says something to her, and Emory turns her head to greet him with a smile. Lila suddenly finds herself hoping that he is the dullest man on the face of the planet, because he's certainly not dull-looking.

Lila's chest tightens, and an awful feeling curls in her stomach. She turns back to the table to grab her drink, but just as she places the glass against her lips, she sees Zoey staring directly at her.

"What's going on over there?" Zoey asks with a grin.

"What do you mean?" Lila asks, though she knows exactly what Zoey is implying.

"You're jealous," Zoey says as she places her elbows on the table, chin propped in her hands.

"And you're drunk," Lila retorts. "The cider has skewed your judgment."

"I'm with Zoey on this one. Can't blame the alcohol for my judgment," Tara says with a laugh.

Lila is jealous, and she knows it. She also knows that whatever was going on between her and Emory last night, Emory regrets it. She thinks it was a mistake.

"Okay, fine!" Lila huffs. "Maybe a little. But it doesn't

matter. Emory doesn't want to go there with me, she practically told me so."

"Oh whatever!" Zoey says loudly, unaware of the fact that the cider has turned up her volume. "She is clearly into you! Will you just tell her how you feel already?" Just as Zoey blurts this out, Lila notices that Emory is heading their way with drinks in hand.

"Shhh," Lila hisses. "She's coming. Chill."

"One cider!" Emory says cheerfully as she passes the glass to Zoey. Lila sees Zoey's eyes dart over to hers with a grin, and she has a feeling that her best friend is about to say something she will not approve of.

"Emory, who was that guy at the bar?" Zoey asks, and Lila glares daggers at Zoey.

"Oh. I'm not sure. Some guy named Will," Emory says casually, as if Will actually was as dull as Lila had hoped.

"He was cute, right?" Zoey says in a high-pitched tone, looking at Lila as if she's telling her she has a plan.

"Yeah, he's fine." Emory says plainly. "Not really my type though."

"Oh? Tall, muscular, and hot isn't your thing?" Zoey asks with a laugh.

"No, I like all those things very much," Emory says with a smile. "Just not on men."

"Ahhhh," Zoey says with a laugh. "Fair enough!" She looks over to Lila as she says this, as if she's nudging her yet again, this time telepathically. Zoey knows Lila is too shy to get to the bottom of Emory's preferences, so she made it her mission to get the question answered.

"Alright, up next we have Lila singing "Silver Springs" by Fleetwood Mac," The announcer calls out to the bar.

"Excuse me, what?!" Lila asks with wide eyes, head cocked to the side as if he has to be joking. Zoey and Tara point to each other with their lips sealed, unwilling to make the real culprit known.

"Get up there, girl!" Emory says as she points to the stage.

"Uh, no fucking way!" Lila says with a dramatic head shake, trying to sink down into her chair.

"Oh come on! Don't keep us waiting!" Emory says loudly, a smirk growing on her face.

"Yeah, I'll get up there when you get up there," Lila retorts with an attitude.

"Alright, let's go," Emory says without hesitation, grabbing Lila's hand and pulling her up from her chair. There is absolutely no way she is doing—

The chimes of Lila's favorite song pour out of the speaker, and she realizes that this is the first time in history that she's unhappy about hearing "Silver Springs." She spends the next five seconds pleading with the universe to somehow make the speaker explode, but she's pulled out of her thoughts when she's handed a microphone.

Emory is lucky that Lila is tipsy, or she would be running off the stage and leaving Emory in the dust. Lila takes a deep breath as the first line of the song approaches, and she finally accepts her fate. With microphones in hand, they start the song.

Lila's voice is initially a whisper, but Emory's smile ignites the bravery she needs to match her volume. Lila is positive that her shaky voice has the mirrors lining the bar on the verge of shattering, but she challenges herself to not care. Lila manages to make it through the first few verses without passing out, and she's coming dangerously close to admitting to herself that this isn't all that bad.

Before she knows it, Lila and Emory are facing each other, belting the bridge of her favorite song. She doesn't care that she's being watched by dozens of people, or even if the mirrors on the bar are shattered to pieces.

There's no song quite as special to Lila as this one, but as she dances with Emory on the stage, she starts to think that this moment might be just as special. Even more so.

The song comes to a close, and Emory puts her hand up in the air towards Lila, ready to give her a high five for their groundbreaking, and possibly mirror-shattering performance. Their hands meet in the air with a clap, but their fingers intertwine loosely as their hands fall back down to their side. The moment is brief, but Lila can feel Emory's fingers graze against her own, as if she's tracing a path up the palm of Lila's hand.

Suddenly remembering they have dozens of eyes on them, their fingers separate, and they swiftly pull their hands back. Lila's fingers are left buzzing, a familiar tingle that's brought on by the sudden absence of Emory's touch.

The buzzing lingers for the rest of their evening, and the terrifying feeling of want in Lila's chest continues to grow.

## CHAPTER SEVENTEEN

"I have a confession," Emory says as Lila pulls their room key out of her pocket, tapping it against the hotel door.

"Oh?" Lila asks in a high-pitched tone, hoping that whatever comes out of Emory's mouth is something along the lines of needing to have Lila, right here and now.

"I know who put your name on the karaoke list."

"No!" Lila gasps as the door opens, welcoming them inside.

"Yep, I do," Emory says as she cocks her head to the side, walking past Lila to take a seat on the bed.

Lila shuts the door behind her, walking over to Emory with her hands on her hips. "Well, are you going to tell me?"

Emory then lifts one of her hands out of her lap, pointing to herself with a flat grin.

"No way!" Lila says with a laugh, genuinely surprised that Zoey wasn't behind it after all.

"Hey, I knew it was your favorite song," Emory says with a shoulder shrug. "I couldn't resist."

"I guess I should have gone with your answer then. Saying I couldn't possibly choose one favorite song."

Lila takes a few steps closer to Emory, and the look in her eye gives her permission to keep stepping closer.

"Well, it's too late now," Emory says confidently, her eyes holding Lila's. Emory then places her hands behind her, leaning back slightly on the bed.

Lila steps forward until her knees are touching Emory's, forcing her legs to part as she steps even closer.

"Well, jokes on you," Lila says softly as she slides a leg between Emory's thighs, causing Emory to let out a hitched breath. Lila moves her hand to Emory's face, tucking a strand of hair behind her ear. "Because I actually had a good time."

Emory lifts her hands from the bed, allowing her body to sit upright, closer to Lila's. She places her hands on the back of Lila's thighs, moving them upward until they disappear just under the hem of Lila's skirt. Lila leans down to close the gap between them, realizing she finally gets to taste the perfect lips she's been staring at all night.

"Wait," Emory says as she turns away, causing Lila's face to fall against her cheek. "I think we should stop."

"Oh." Lila steps back from Emory, jarred from the whiplash of almost having Emory's lips against hers. She can't help but feel a little embarrassed, practically jumping Emory the moment they stepped into their hotel room. "Um, yeah, no problem."

"It's not that I don't want to Lila," Emory says, meeting Lila's eyes. "Trust me, I do. It's all I've been thinking about. Honestly, I don't think I ever stop thinking about it. Hell, I jumped at the chance last night when I thought it was what you wanted. But I shouldn't have."

"Oh," Lila says, pausing as she tries to make sense of what Emory is saying. "I'm okay with anything you want. But if you want to, or if you want me…then why are we stopping?"

Emory pulls her gaze away from Lila's, and her eyes find a comfortable resting place on the floor. Emory clears her throat as she brings her hands back to her lap, her nerves obvious as she continues. "I can't get wrapped up in something complicated Lila."

"I understand that," Lila says with a confused tone, unsure

of how this applies to their situation.

Emory lifts her head again, feeling brave enough to meet Lila's eyes. "And I don't do casual. It just doesn't work for me."

Now Lila is really confused. What makes Emory assume that Lila is only interested in something casual? "I don't understand what you mean by complicated...or by casual," Lila says as she draws her eyebrows together. "I don't under—"

"Look," Emory interrupts. "I saw you and Dr. Hale in the parking lot the other day, and I don't want to get wrapped up in this if you are back together. Even if you are just sleeping together and you're keeping your options open, whatever it is, it's just not something I'm interested in."

"Wait," Lila says as she processes Emory's words.

"I know we just met, but I cannot get you out of my head Lila. Ever since that night at Patty's, I can't stop wondering what it would be like to be with you," Emory says, her voice strained with each word. "I know me, and if we go there....If this is going to be complicated, then I just need to back out now."

Lila thinks back to the moment she spent talking to Arthur about the situation with Phoebe's parents. She was just helping him work through his feelings, so she can't imagine why Emory would think—wait. Lila recalls the moment Arthur placed his hand on her cheek. She remembers finding Emory in the breakroom when she came inside, the breakroom with the giant window that faces the parking lot. *Of course.*

"Oh my gosh," Lila says in a regretful tone. "Emory, no. I promise it's not what you think." Emory continues to look at Lila, begging for her to explain it without saying the words. "I understand why you would think that, but I shut it down with him—immediately."

"He was just having a hard time after talking to Phoebe's parents, and I was helping him work through an anxiety attack. He got the wrong idea for just a second, but..." Lila pauses as she steps toward Emory again, grabbing one of her hands and placing it in her own.

"I promise. There is nothing going on between Arthur and I." Lila squeezes Emory's hand, hoping she believes every word of what she's saying. "And I don't do casual either. Especially not with you."

Lila feels Emory slipping her hand out of Lila's grasp, and for a moment, she thinks she's about to pull away completely. But in an instant, the hand Lila was holding is now tugging on her shirt, drawing her into Emory's body with a swift, desperate motion. It reminds Lila of being in Emory's arms just last night, knowing now that Emory was dying to have her, just as much as she wanted Emory.

Lila straddles Emory on the edge of the bed as they crash into each other, and it feels as if another layer between them has finally peeled away. Lila tilts her face to meet Emory's lips, and when they finally touch, the feeling is electric. Emory's hands are now traveling down Lila's back, only stopping to grip Lila's shirt in a hungry need to pull her closer. Lila sinks into her straddle to deepen their kiss, sliding her fingers through Emory's thick hair.

She tugs on the luxurious locks between her fingers, tilting Emory's head back so she can better explore their kiss. Emory tastes like mint and the sweet juice she mixed with her liquor, and Lila can't get enough. Emory releases a soft moan as their tongues graze against each other, and Lila swears it's the most beautiful sound she's ever heard. Just as Lila takes Emory's bottom lip between her teeth, Emory slides both of her hands up Lila's skirt, squeezing her ass like a woman deprived.

"You have no idea how badly I've wanted my hands on you," Emory says as she pulls her lips away from Lila's, turning her focus to Lila's neck. Emory traces a path of hungry kisses from Lila's jaw line to her collarbone, stopping just as her lips meet the boundary of Lila's t-shirt. Emory pulls on Lila's shirt to expose more of her neck, but Lila needs more. She sits back in her straddle and reaches for the bottom of her shirt, pulling it up and over her head in a smooth motion.

Emory's eyes fall to the cleavage pouring out of Lila's lacy pink bra, and Lila's skin burns at the need in Emory's eyes. Lila grabs Emory's hands and moves them up to the swell of her breasts, just as she says, "Show me how bad you've wanted me then."

Something ignites in Emory, and she wastes no time wrapping her arm around Lila's lower back, swinging her around until her back hits the mattress.

Lila takes a ragged breath as she looks up at Emory, unable to take her eyes off the stunning woman that's exploring her body. Emory's lips fall to Lila's stomach with pure need, tracing wet kisses down to her navel. Just as her hands find their way back up to Lila's breasts—

*KNOCK, KNOCK, KNOCK.*

Lila and Emory freeze, unsure of whether or not the knocking is coming from their door or their neighbor's. Lila's heart is beating out of her chest, and she wonders if Emory can feel her racing heart now that her hands are no longer busy.

"Hey, it's Zoey," they hear calling out from the hallway. "We got pizza!"

Their heads fall with frustration, and Lila realizes that this may be the only time she is actually annoyed by her best friend's presence. Emory lifts her head from Lila's shoulder and releases a breath, equally disappointed by the interruption.

"Is she still your favorite person?" Lila says with a painful laugh, wishing she could somehow turn back time.

"This is definitely a strike against our friendship," Emory says as she pulls herself from Lila's body and shifts back onto her heels, tossing Lila the shirt she threw over her head in a fever. Emory walks to the door while Lila gets dressed, opening the door once Lila gives her a nod.

"There's a 24/7 pizza shop one road over!" Zoey says as she walks into the room with two big pizza boxes in hand. "I'm officially moving here!"

Tara trails in behind her with a smaller box, saying, "And they had vegan slices!"

Zoey sits down next to Lila on the bed, opening the pizza boxes to display their late night feast. Lila is still annoyed by the night's sudden change in trajectory, but she can't deny how amazing the pizza looks. Tara and Emory sit on the other end of the bed, and Zoey spreads the boxes out to let everyone grab a piece.

As the minutes pass, Lila wonders if everyone in the room can feel the shift in the air each time her gaze meets Emory's. Each glance shares a secret, and she's positive the room heats as her mind travels back in time, when Emory's lips were trailing down her stomach.

"I don't know about you guys," Zoey says with a mouth full of pizza. "But this was definitely one of the best conferences I've been to! We'll have to come to this one again next year!"

"You know I'm down! But I mean, is it really fair to compare it to our last conference experience?" Tara asks.

"Okay, fair point." Zoey laughs.

"Why, what was so bad about your last conference?" Emory asks as she looks to Tara.

"Oh god," Lila laughs. "It was an actual nightmare. Like so bad it was comical."

"Alright, I have to know now," Emory laughs.

"Well, we began our trip with a very car sick Zoey," Lila laughs. "We made the drive to Houston for this one, and we had to pull over to let Zoey puke every 30 minutes."

"Hey!" Zoey interrupts. "It's not like that affected all of you! I was the one suffering."

"It did the first time when you missed your barf bag and puked all over the front seat." Tara laughs. "I had to do everything in my power to not puke all over the car myself!"

"You deal with animal vomit and blood daily, but you can't handle a little human vomit?" Zoey retorts. "Come on!"

"Yeah, there's a reason I didn't go into human nursing." Tara laughs. "People are gross, and I love you, but your vomit was gross."

"And then when we finally made it there and got some rest for the conference, we woke up in the morning and discovered that my car was towed!" Lila says. "I had to miss the first couple lectures to go get my car out of jail."

"Oh man," Emory laughs. "That is pretty bad."

"I wish we could say that was it," Zoey adds as she scrunches her eyebrows together. "It gets worse."

"Yeah, the conference gave us all a lovely parting gift," Lila says with a pause. "COVID. We were down for days."

"Yeah, we all suffered through it together at Lila's place. Oliver was happy to have a variety of warm bodies to lay on, at least!" Tara laughs.

"Well, I think we can all see who the good luck charm is in this equation," Emory says as she points to herself.

"For real!" Zoey says. "Looks like you're stuck with us Emory."

Emory glances over to Lila as Zoey says the words, and Lila hopes she really will stick around for a while, maybe even forever.

Their 3 a.m. pizza delivery turned into a Grey's Anatomy marathon, three of them huddled up on the bed and Tara on the couch. Zoey slept on the edge of the bed so she could easily reach the plug and charge her phone, leaving Lila and Emory lying beside each other. Their steamy moment from earlier may have been interrupted, but Lila can feel the sizzling heat that still lingers between them.

Emory's hand finds its way to Lila's as they close their eyes, and their fingers come together like an anchor, holding them still in this moment. Lila drifts to sleep with the sounds of her favorite characters playing in the background, heart absolutely full.

# CHAPTER EIGHTEEN

Lila is still recovering from their karaoke filled night in Austin. She swears her hangovers took on a new form when she turned 28, and it seems like they've only gotten worse in the year that's followed. Now, here she is almost 48 hours later, feeling the twinge of a lingering headache the moment she wakes up.

The only one that has been pleased about Lila's suffering is Oliver, because Lila became one with her couch the moment she got home Thursday afternoon. Clearly making up for two days of cuddle deprivation, Oliver took this opportunity to plant himself firmly on her chest, only budging now at the sound of her morning alarm.

Lila rolls over to disable her incessant alarm, and she discovers that she's not the only one that's been horizontal since they've returned home.

EMORY

I have been unconscious for 14 hours.

EMORY

Why am I still exhausted?

She smiles at her screen, understanding exactly how

Emory is feeling right now. At least Lila got to enjoy two more hours of sleep than Emory did, a fact that she will certainly rub in once she sees her.

LILA

> Please tell me that I have a relaxing day ahead with only mildly ill patients?

EMORY

> You and I are just getting started. You want me to start lying to you already?

LILA

> *screaming into my pillow*

A full parking lot at 10 a.m. on a Friday is never a good sign. Her suspicions of a stressful shift ahead are confirmed when she's asked to take over a room the moment she walks in the door, before she's even had a chance to clock in. There's no sign of Emory, so she must be tucked away in a room with a new patient.

"Sorry to throw this at you the moment you walk in," Susan says apologetically. "There's a dog in room three with bloody urine. Can you take over? She's already checked in and ready for x-rays."

"Sure thing," Lila says with a head nod. "What's her name?"

"Bella!"

*The first Bella of the day, but certainly not the last.*

"Thanks Lila! Let me know when you're ready in x-ray, and I'll come help."

Lila puts her things away quickly, and she heads into room three to collect the first of many Bellas she'll meet this weekend. She's the epitome of a crusty white dog, but even with a painful belly, she walks to Lila with a happy tail wag. She's an absolute sweetheart, so she won't hold her crusty eyes and generic name against her—this time.

Lila and Susan get Bella on to the x-ray table and lay her on her side, Bella licking Lila's hand as she holds her still.

"How was the conference?" Susan asks. "Did you have fun?"

*Lila and Emory sure did. Or, almost did.*

"Yeah! It was a blast actually," Lila says with a smile. "Emory's really great."

"See, I knew you two would get along!"

Moments after they click the x-ray pedal, the cause of Bella's bloody urine is glaring back at them on the computer screen.

"Woah!" Lila says with a gasp. "That's an impressive bladder stone!"

"It's almost as big as her, poor thing," Susan says with a sigh, knowing that surgery is in this little one's near future.

"I'll go get her set up in a cage. Can you send her films over?" Susan asks as she scoops Bella into her arms, leaving the room with the crusty white pup in tow.

Lila steps over to the x-ray monitor to do as Susan asked, but just as she hits send, Lila hears the door shut behind her. Before she can turn her body to see who it is, she feels two hands wrap around her waist, and a familiar voice in her ear.

"I thought I heard you in here," Emory says in Lila's ear. She places a soft kiss on her neck, and Lila feels chills dance across her body.

"Susan snagged me the moment I walked in the door," Lila answers, closing her eyes as Emory's breath tickles her neck.

"Do you have plans tomorrow?" Emory asks as she removes her wandering hands from Lila's waist, placing them on the counter in front of them. Lila is now encased between Emory's arms, feeling the warmth of her body pressed up against hers.

"Well, I always spend time with Zoey on Saturday, but I'm sure she won't mind if we cut the day short." Lila turns her head to get a glimpse of Emory behind her, her lips just inches away from hers now.

"Oh, I know she won't mind," Emory says with a soft laugh.

"And why's that?" Lila asks as she turns around, finally locking eyes with Emory.

"Because she traded shifts with me so I can take you on a date," Emory says with a cocky smile.

"Wait," Lila pauses, processing the fact that Zoey is in on this plan. "She did?"

"Mhm." Emory's dimple is the star of the show now. "So, I'll pick you up at 12?"

"Oh, this is a full day affair?" Lila asks as she cocks her head to the side.

Emory slides her hands further onto the counter and leans in closer to Lila, pushing her back up against the counter behind her.

"I want you to myself all day," Emory says as she brings her lips dangerously close to Lila's. "But I also want you to myself all night."

Lila's knees practically buckle, and she forces out a ragged breath. She's dangerously close to pouncing on Emory in the fucking x-ray room, but just before she loses all control, Emory places a kiss on her forehead and backs away. She's out of the room just as quickly as she swooped in, leaving Lila in a dizzying trance.

Lila hasn't just been swept up in the Emory allure, she has been swallowed whole. There's no going back.

## CHAPTER NINETEEN

As tempting as it is to go for some variation of her standard comfort outfit, Lila pushes her band tees aside, reaching further into her closet for something different. Lila doesn't usually get too worked up about a first date, but just as she has with any other activity involving Emory, she's feeling nervous.

All she knows about the date Emory has planned is that it's something Emory has never done before, and that she wants her first time to be with Lila. The thought of someone planning an actual date for her is dizzying enough, let alone the idea that Emory wants to experience something new with her for the first time.

The bar is shockingly low for Lila when it comes to dating and any effort put into the experience, but it still feels special. Lila is usually the one making the plans and dragging her partner along, but look at her now, wrapped up in someone that actually seems to give a shit.

There's a knock at the door, and Lila's stomach suddenly feels fluttery. She can't even remember the last time this sensation churned in her belly, a combination of excitement and nerves swirling around as one.

Lila opens the door to find Emory standing on the other

side of it, pulling an unexpected gift out from behind her back.

"Hey!" Lila says just as she sees the pot in Emory's hands. "Is that…cat grass?"

"It sure is," Emory answers with a soft smile as she hands the pot over to Lila. "Zoey said you're not big on flowers."

Lila laughs as she takes the pot from Emory's hands. "I love that this was your next jump from flowers."

"I've always heard the way to a woman's heart is through her cat." Just as Emory says it, Lila's eyebrows scrunch, letting out an awkward laugh as she shakes her head.

"Yeah, I didn't like that the moment I said it," Emory says with a chuckle. "Are you ready to go?"

Lila's fluttering stomach suddenly calms, knowing whatever is ahead, it will be perfect.

∼

"There he is, in all his glory," Lila says as she points up to the creepy statue dressed in a cowboy hat.

"You know, I don't know what I was expecting, but it wasn't that." Emory stares up at the massive Texas State Fair icon, known as Big Tex. "He's kind of scary."

"Oh, he's terrifying," Lila says with a laugh. "But this new Big Tex isn't as scary as the original one."

"Wait, you're telling me that I'm looking at an imposter?" Emory asks as she points to the structure towering above her.

"Oh my god, yeah. The original Big Tex lost his life in a fiery blaze," Lila says as she nods her head, as if she's telling the story of a great loss. "It was a sad day in Texas history."

Emory nods as she looks the horrifying mascot in the eye. "How did the community handle that?"

"Well, we came together and we pushed through."

"Wow," Emory says as she turns her head away from Big Tex and looks at Lila. "I have chills."

Lila laughs as she nudges Emory's arm, Emory bumping hers right back.

"Alright!" Emory says as she claps her hands together. "What should we do first?"

"Well," Lila says. "I think we have to do the Ferris wheel."

"Ooh, I've always wanted to make out at the top of a Ferris wheel."

"Eh, I've done it," Lila says with a shoulder shrug. "It's overrated."

"Well, that's only because you've never done it with me," Emory says with a cocky smile as she leans into Lila.

The Ferris wheel line is as long as it always is, but this is the first time Lila doesn't mind waiting. People watching with Emory might just be her new favorite activity.

It's finally their turn to ditch the people watching and hop onto the Ferris wheel. Lila and Emory step into the egg-shaped cage and sit side by side, Lila taking this opportunity to reach over and grab Emory's hand.

"In just a few minutes you'll be living out your Ferris wheel fantasy," Lila says as her and Emory lock eyes, seconds away from closing the gap between them when—

A man and a small child step into the cage with them, and the man helps the little boy up onto the seat before sitting down himself.

"Hey there," the man says with a small nod. Lila and Emory smile back at him politely.

The Ferris wheel begins to rock as they move forward, and Emory leans over to whisper in Lila's ear. "Well this is not how my fantasy went."

~

They spend the next five hours taking advantage of everything the Texas State Fair has to offer. They eat copious amounts of fried food, ride carnival rides until they almost vomit, and they drain every last point on their game cards.

This may not be Lila's first Texas State Fair experience, or anywhere near it for that matter. But somehow, it still feels new. Like she's taking it in for the very first time, right along with Emory.

Lila catches herself smiling on the ride back to her place as she thinks about how perfect of a day it was. But, it's not just today that has her grinning like an idiot. It's everything, right now. Not long ago they were arguing over spilled coffee and catheter dating, but here they are now, sitting next to each other in post-date bliss.

Before she has a chance to wipe the evidence of disgusting happiness off her face, Emory spots it.

"What are you smiling about over there?" Emory asks, breaking the comfortable silence in the car.

"I'm not sure what you're talking about," Lila says coyly, cheeks immediately turning a shade of red.

"Mhmm," Emory says sarcastically, looking back at the road ahead.

Lila isn't sure why she's embarrassed to announce her current state of contentment. It seems like Emory is just as happy as she is, so why does admitting it out loud feel so impossible?

Maybe it's the fact that she's only known this woman for two weeks, and falling this hard for someone you barely know is silly. Ridiculous even. A one way ticket to heartbreak.

Admitting it to herself is one thing, but saying it out loud is another. Lila keeps her lips sealed about her fluttering heart the entire ride home.

## CHAPTER TWENTY

"What if he doesn't like me?" Emory asks as she follows Lila up the stairs and down the hall to her apartment door.

"Well, then this ends right here and now," Lila says quickly, knowing that Oliver is the most easy going cat on the planet and will be pleased to have another admirer.

Lila unlocks her door and pushes it open, and just as he always does, Oliver runs to greet her with a raspy meow. He pauses for a second as he looks up at Emory with slight confusion, likely due to the fact that it's been months since anyone other than Zoey walked through Lila's door.

Emory squats down and holds her hand out to Oliver, and just as Lila thought, Oliver rubs his head against her hand without hesitation.

"Alright, looks like you passed," Lila says with a smile, wondering if Emory truly was nervous about getting her cat's approval. "Though, I can't say it means much. He liked my exes as well."

"Ah! Very reassuring, thank you." Emory laughs as she scratches Oliver's chin.

Lila sets her purse down on her dining room chair, and as she turns back to face Emory, she is already standing up and moving towards her. Emory reaches down to grab Lila's hand, and their fingers intertwine as if they have done this a million times before. Lila raises her gaze from their laced fingers to meet Emory's eyes, and it feels like her entire body is coming apart.

Emory's eyes flick down to Lila's lips before coming back again, and Lila realizes that she's asking for permission, making sure she still wants this just as bad as she did in that hotel room. Lila lifts her other hand and traces a path up Emory's body, not stopping until her hand has a soft grasp on the back of Emory's neck. Lila pulls Emory in slowly, finally closing the unbearable gap between them.

The kiss they shared just a few days ago felt frenzied, charged with pure need and alcohol. But this one feels different. It seems curious and explorative, as if Emory wants to taste every inch of her without missing a thing. Lila opens her mouth wider to deepen their kiss, her entire body loosening under Emory's touch.

Lila curves her body so she can better align with Emory's, trying to get as close to this incredible woman as possible. As if she can sense how desperate Lila is to fit against her body, Emory lifts Lila off the ground, setting her down on the dining table behind them.

Lila's legs spread the moment she hits the table, and Emory fits between her legs like a missing puzzle piece. Their mouths meet again, but this time, the kiss is hungry and greedy. Lila's hands tangle in Emory's hair, craving every single inch of Emory's body. As if Emory could read her thoughts, Emory tugs on Lila's sweater, pulling it over her head without a hitch. Lila then unclasps her bra in a fluid motion, letting it fall to the floor in a slowly growing pile of tossed aside clothes.

Emory's eyes fall to Lila's chest, and the pure need in her eyes sends chills down Lila's entire body. Just as Emory is about to put her lips against Lila's sternum and get a taste, Lila leans back and says, "I need to see you too."

Emory's lips turn into a sexy grin, and she pulls her shirt over her head, revealing a pink bra that's completely sheer. Lila can see Emory's nipples and she can't fight the immediate pull to reach up and touch Emory's skin. Lila's hands travel to the swell of Emory's breasts, and as Lila marvels at Emory's incredible body, Emory unclasps her bra.

Lila moves her hands to let the lace slide down Emory's arms and off her body, revealing the most gorgeous sight Lila has ever seen. Lila brings her hands back up to cup Emory's breasts, letting her thumbs tease her nipples with a soft graze.

"Your body is perfect," Lila says as her eyes meet Emory's, her fingers teasing her nipples with a soft tug. Something in Lila's words sends Emory into a craze, and she pushes Lila backwards until her elbows meet the table, her back almost flat against the wood.

"Can I take these off?" Emory asks as she reaches for the buttons on Lila's jeans.

"Hell yes!" Lila responds. Emory unzips Lila's pants and moves them down her hips, Lila raising slightly off the table to let Emory remove them completely. Lila kicks the jeans off once they reach her ankles, and she can feel Emory's pause.

"Oh my god," Emory exclaims as she looks down at Lila's body, her eyes traveling across every inch of her skin. Suddenly feeling slightly self-conscious, Lila props herself up on her hands, looking at Emory as she takes in what she sees.

"Um," Lila says softly. "Is everything okay?"

Emory's eyes dart back up to Lila's as she says, "Are you kidding? I'm more than okay. You have no idea how sexy you are."

"Oh," Lila says with a soft exhale.

"Can I please taste you?" Emory asks. "I've been dying to all day."

Hearing Emory say those words has Lila melting, but she manages to say, "yes, please."

Emory wastes absolutely no time once she gets confirmation from Lila. Her mouth begins an incredible trail down

Lila's body. She kisses the underside of her breast, licking upward until her tongue sweeps across Lila's nipple, taking it in her mouth completely. Lila lets out a moan that has been buried deep in her chest, a part of her only Emory can awaken. Her tongue goes on a journey to her other nipple, in between her breasts, down her stomach, and finally, dangerously close to the part of her body that craves Emory most.

Emory begins to leave a trail of kisses down Lila's thigh, stopping just shy of where she aches. Emory finally curls a finger under the waistband of Lila's panties, pulling them down as she continues to tease her thighs with licks and kisses. Lila lifts her ass off the table so Emory can get her naked, more eager than ever to have Emory's incredible mouth on her body.

Down on her knees, Emory is now at the perfect height to taste Lila. Emory looks up at Lila as she parts her legs, and Lila feels like she's going to explode. How the hell did Lila get so lucky? To have this incredible woman between her thighs, practically begging to make her cum.

Lila practically bucks off the table as Emory parts her with her fingers, massaging her clit before diving in with gentle kisses. She is soft with her touch at first, teasing Lila with gentle friction. But once Lila buries her fingers in Emory's hair, moaning at her touch, Emory doesn't hold back any longer.

Emory drags her tongue from Lila's entrance to her clit, finally applying the suction Lila craves. Emory takes turns licking and sucking where Lila needs it most, and Lila is on the verge of coming undone beneath her touch. Lila's thighs begin to tremble, and just when she thinks it can't get any better, Emory pushes a finger inside of Lila, pumping her finger as her tongue continues to work.

It doesn't take long for Lila to break, pleasure building between her legs that is unlike anything she has experienced before. Lila's legs clench around Emory's head, nails digging into Emory's back as she cries out in pure bliss. Lila rides the waves of pleasure until it's too much to bear, finally pulling Emory back up her body to meet her eyes.

Emory is obviously loving every second of this, sporting a smug grin that's almost too adorable to handle. "Good?" Emory asks as she's face to face with Lila again, knowing just how good she was by the sounds she pulled out of Lila.

Still reeling from the most mind-blowing orgasm she's ever had, she manages to sit up quickly, hopping down from the table where she just had her world rocked. Lila grabs Emory by the waist of her jeans, pulling her along as she walks backwards down the hall and into her room. Lila turns Emory around once they reach the bedroom, pushing her backwards until she falls onto Lila's bed.

"Now it's my turn to make you cum," Lila says as she looks down at Emory, ready to climb on top of her body. Emory scoots back until she is propped up by the pile of pillows near Lila's headboard, allowing her to watch Lila's every move. Lila crawls to Emory on her hands and knees, stopping once she makes contact with the buttons on Emory's jeans.

"Um, why are these still on?" Lila asks in a playful tone as she unzips Emory's pants, pulling them down her thighs as quickly as she possibly can. Her bare legs reveal a beautiful tattoo of flowers and vines, the artwork traveling up her thigh and around her hip. Some of the design is tucked away under a pair of lacy pink panties, just as sheer as the bra Lila peeled off Emory minutes earlier.

The realization that Emory is in her bed nearly naked makes Lila feel momentarily dazed, but once the world comes back into focus, she climbs up Emory's body until she's straddling her thighs. Lila's lips find their way to Emory's neck, and she wastes no time placing hungry kisses on her skin.

With her mouth busy against Emory's neck, she starts exploring every inch of Emory's beautiful body with her hands. Lila traces her fingers slowly down Emory's body, and she feels Emory's body erupt in chills beneath her touch. She picks up where she left off when she first removed Emory's bra, just before Emory took over and sent Lila to the moon. Lila's thumbs trace soft circles around her nipple, then to the other, teasing her until her back is arching off the bed.

Lila moves her mouth from Emory's neck and back to her lips, tongues twirling against each other like a beautiful dance. Lila walks her fingers down Emory's stomach, further and further until she hits a boundary of lace.

"May I?" Lila asks just before she dips her hand under the sheer lace and between Emory's thighs. Emory pauses their kiss to growl out a "please," and the tone in Emory's voice sends a shock of electricity through her body. The feeling of Emory wet beneath her is everything she's been fantasizing about. Lila runs her finger up and down the length of Emory, moving back up to her clit to rub delicious circles.

Emory pulls away from their kiss and turns her head, filling Lila's ear with the most sensual moans. Lila wants Emory to come undone beneath her, so she slides her fingers down Emory's wet heat, inserting a finger, then two. Emory arches into the pressure of Lila's fingers, riding her with every single thrust. All she wants to do is make this beautiful woman scream, so Lila moves her thumb back up to Emory's clit, swirling gently as her other fingers continue to work. She can feel Emory's body beginning to melt, fingers digging into her back as her moans pick up speed. It's not long before Emory is coming undone beneath her, moaning a variety of obscenities as the pleasure moves through her body. Lila watches Emory's face through it all, and she swears it's the most beautiful thing she's ever seen.

∽

Lila and Emory lay curled up in a pile of blankets and pillows, still riding the high of their perfect day. There's an ease between them that Lila can't explain, but she wants to hold on to this feeling as long as she can.

"Remind me again to thank Zoey for switching shifts with me," Emory says with a laugh as she rolls over, placing a gentle kiss on Lila's lips.

"Zoey was probably sick of hearing me pine over you," Lila smiles as she pulls away from Emory's lips. "It was purely selfish, I'm sure."

"Who would have thought I'd be going out of my way to take the clinic bully on a date," Emory teases with a smirk and Lila immediately pushes her shoulder in retaliation.

"I'm so—"

"I'm kidding, please don't apologize again," Emory says with a laugh, as Lila has apologized at least twice a day since they started getting to know each other better.

"But, in all seriousness," Emory starts and then pauses, taking a breath before she continues. "I'm really glad this happened." Emory strokes Lila's hair as she says the words, and Lila searches for Emory's other hand to hold.

"I was in a pretty bad place when I got here. Starting over is scary...but you've made it easier. Zoey and Tara have too, in different ways, of course." Lila squeezes Emory's hand. "I'm glad I have all of you now."

Lila pulls her hand from Emory's, rolling her body so she can prop herself on Emory's chest and face her. "We're glad we have you too," Lila replies with a smile.

"Um, I don't know if this is the best time to ask," Lila says tentatively. "But, I would really love to know what happened back in Seattle, if you're willing to share it with me."

Emory goes still for a moment, and Lila immediately regrets saying the words. She's sure that she's just tainted their perfect day together with her prying curiosity, but to her surprise, Emory starts to share.

"Well, I had a group of close friends back in Seattle that I met in college. There were four of us, and we were pretty much inseparable. Erin, Becca, and Avery." Lila squeezes Emory's hand, trying to offer her subtle comfort as she continues. "We all remained best friends after we graduated, but

Erin and I started spending a lot of time together. We started dating."

"Things were really great for a while. We moved in together after a couple years, and I just thought everything was perfect." Emory pauses for a second, and Lila can tell it's painful for Emory to relive. "Until I came home one evening and Erin and Avery were sitting on the couch, and I could tell they were both really nervous. They told me that about a year into Erin and I's relationship, they started sleeping together for a short period. They said it only happened a handful of times, that they knew it was wrong, and they ended it soon after it began."

Lila feels a sudden ache in her chest, unable to imagine what that kind of betrayal feels like.

"They told me there had been nothing between them since, and that they didn't want to ruin our friendships over something that meant nothing in the long run. I wondered why they were even telling me, why they had the sudden change of heart....but then I found out that they were only coming clean because Becca's long-term boyfriend found out about it, and he was threatening to tell me himself."

Lila squeezes Emory's hand again.

"Erin didn't understand why I couldn't get over it and why I was letting this be the end of us when we had come so far since then. But I couldn't look at her the same way. Avery either. It was too much."

"I moved out a month later, I told Erin and Avery that I wanted nothing to do with them, and I tried to start over the best I could. I cut them out of my life completely, but it felt impossible to move forward. There were reminders everywhere, even in my friendship with Becca. She of course had no idea either, but she was more inclined to believe their apologies and forgive them, but I just couldn't."

"So when Susan heard about what was happening and offered me a way out, I knew I had to go for it. I had lived in

Seattle my whole life, so it felt crazy to even consider, but something in my gut said I needed to at least try."

Emory was staring at the ceiling throughout her sharing, but once she finished, she finally looked back down at Lila.

"I'm so sorry that happened to you Emory," Lila says, holding Emory's gaze. "But, I'm so proud of you for taking a chance and exploring a new path. Not many people could do that. I don't think I could."

Lila didn't think it was possible to admire Emory more than she already did for packing up her life and starting over, but now, after hearing everything she's been through, she's blown away.

"You really are incredible, you know?" Lila says softly, hoping Emory can see just how amazing she really is.

Lila feels Emory soften beneath her, as if sharing her story with Lila finally gives her body permission to deflate. They stay wrapped up in their oasis of pillows and blankets, allowing themselves to be overtaken by whatever this is.

## CHAPTER TWENTY-ONE

Lila woke in the morning to the feeling of Emory's hand on her cheek, saying goodbye to her so she could head back to her place and get ready for work. It took Lila some time to pull herself out of the sleep and sex induced haze Emory left her in—or more like the sex and no-sleep induced haze. Their hands found their way back to each other's bodies in the middle of the night, eager to learn more about the other's touch.

A night with Emory was certainly worth her current state of sleep deprivation, but she is paying for it now as she pulls into work, completely exhausted and craving more sleep. She practically stumbles through the door and into the clinic, but a wave of relief washes over her when she realizes it's actually not that busy—for once in the history of all Sundays. She doesn't dare say it out loud though.

"Good morning!" Lila hears a cheerful voice creep up next to her as she clocks in, one that belongs to her best friend and undercover matchmaker. Sure, Zoey didn't do all the work in getting her and Emory together, but it was still an undercover operation Lila was briefly unaware of.

"So," Zoey says as she places her elbows on the desk next

to Lila, putting her chin in her hands as if playing innocent. "Are you and Emory in love?"

"Girl," Lila says with a laugh as she nudges her best friend.

"Fine, but I want all the details later," Zoey retorts with a smirk as she walks away, likely already knowing that Lila is in deep.

Lila turns to step away from the computer, but as she does, she sees Arthur, a few feet away from her flipping through a surgery book. He's close enough that he must have heard her and Zoey's brief chat, but if that's the case, he's not showing any sign of emotion.

Lila thinks back to Arthur snapping at her just a few weeks ago when Zoey mentioned a date, so this feels like major progress. Their curbside chat last week may have almost tampered with her and Emory, but maybe it's what Arthur needed to finally close that door.

Lila is snapped to attention by the sound of an exam room door opening, and out walks Emory, looking as good as ever. Lila can't comprehend how she still looks flawless after a sleepless night, especially since Lila had to apply two layers of concealer to hide her dark circles this morning. Emory disappears around the corner, and though Lila holds off for a second before running over to say hello, she quickly caves into her giddiness and walks her way.

"Hey you," Lila says as she walks up to Emory, currently in the process of filling a long line of prescriptions.

"Hey!" Emory says with a smile, proving to be just as giddy as Lila. "Are you as exhausted as I am?"

"I'm bordering on delirious," Lila answers with a laugh.

"Well, that means we did good then," Emory says with a smirk, holding her hand up to give Lila a high five.

Lila high fives Emory to signify their good work and they laugh together in their unified cheesiness.

"Emory," Dr. Hale's voice cuts through the sound of their laughter. "They just approved the surgery. Can you start getting set up? I want to get it done now in case it gets busy later."

"Yeah, of course," Emory answers. The moment feels a little uncomfortable for Lila, but neither Arthur or Emory show any sign of feeling the same.

"What's the surgery?" Lila asks.

"It's for Bella, the one with the bladder stones. They just needed a day to work out the payment, but she's back and good to go now."

"Oh, great!" Lila says with a smile. "I'm so glad."

"I'm going to go get set up!"

∼

"Okay, that's weird," Zoey says as she walks up to Lila, both of them looking into the surgical suite.

Not only is it awkward enough to see Emory and Arthur, both people who have seen Lila naked—one as recently as last night—working in a small room together. But they aren't just working, they're having a good time.

It looks like they're engaged in a full-blown conversation, Arthur even letting out a few ridiculous laughs. The surgical suite is completely silent when Lila and Arthur are held captive together in it, and then there's Arthur and Emory, laughing as if they are old pals.

"Right?" Lila says with a laugh as she continues to watch them. "I've never seen him this chatty in there. With anyone!"

"Think they're comparing notes?" Zoey says sarcastically.

"God, I didn't even consider that possibility," Lila says as she looks on in horror.

"So, that means Emory has notes to compare then?" Zoey asks with a grin, already knowing the answer.

Lila rolls her eyes as she looks over to Zoey, sporting a look that very obviously says 'duh'.

"God," Lila huffs as she looks back over at Arthur and

Emory, chatting as if they actually enjoy each other's company. "I hate this."

~

The shockingly quiet shift soon turned into what's usually expected of a Sunday at the ER. Dr. Hale and Emory are lucky they went to surgery when they did, because shit absolutely hit the fan soon after they finished.

Not only did shit figuratively hit the fan, but it was incredibly likely that there was actual shit scattered across the clinic. Everything that walked through the doors had diarrhea, and Lila felt like she was on a constant cleaning rotation all day.

"I cannot wait to be unconscious," Emory says to Lila as she clocks out, finally wrapping up her shift and this shit storm of a day. Lila still has a few more hours of her shift, and she is dreading every moment of it.

"God, I hope I'm soon behind you," Lila responds, equally as drained as Emory. "I'll walk you out."

"I'll be right back!" Lila calls out to Zoey and Tara as she walks around the corner with Emory. "By the way," Lila says quietly as they open the back door and step out into the parking lot. "You and Arthur seemed very chummy in your surgery."

"Did we now?" Emory asks with a sarcastic grin, fully aware that this is driving Lila crazy.

"Mhmm," Lila says. "What were you guys cackling about?"

"Wouldn't you like to know?" Emory retorts with a laugh. Just as Lila is about to give her an equally hard time, Emory's body stiffens, and Lila watches her carefree face turn shockingly cold.

"Erin?" Emory asks with a mixture of shock and confusion. Lila turns to see a petite girl with blonde hair on the other end of the parking lot, standing nervously next to Emory's car.

"What are you doing here?" Emory's tone is cold, and Lila

realizes that she's never heard Emory speak this way. Even when she was arguing with Lila across the clinic about patient care and catheter dates, it was nothing like this.

"Hi, um—" the woman starts and then stops, obviously equally taken aback by Emory's shortness. "I came here to talk. Can we please talk?"

"You're waiting for me in my work parking lot? In Texas? Way to corner me into a conversation Erin!" Emory snaps, and Lila's discomfort grows by the second. She's not sure if she should run away or stay here in support of Emory, but her visceral discomfort immobilizes her instead.

"Um, I'm sorry, maybe I should—" Lila interrupts quietly, unsure of what to do with herself during this painfully unpleasant moment.

"Lila, god, I'm sorry." Emory turns to face her, rubbing her hands along her face with radiating frustration. "Fuck, what am I supposed to do with this?"

Lila dips her hands into her scrub pockets, unsure of how to handle this. Lila glances back and forth between Emory and Erin, both women visibly shaken by the weight of this moment.

"Um…..maybe you should just go talk to her," Lila says. Emory lifts her head from the ground to meet Lila's eyes. "If she came this far to see you, she's probably not going to leave until she says what she needs to say."

Emory looks back down at the ground as she processes this situation, shaking her head as she lets out a frustrated sigh. Lila can see Emory's deep, visceral pain with each second that passes. "Okay," Emory says as she lets out a sigh. " You're right. I'll see what the hell it is that she wants."

A few moments pass, both of them unsure of what to say.

"I'll come over after I talk to her. Is that okay?" Emory asks. "It won't be long. I'm not giving her much of my time."

"Yes, of course," Lila answers softly. "I'll be home in a bit. Do what you need to do."

Lila watches Emory walk off, directing Erin to follow her

as she gets into her car. Emory's icy demeanor holds strong as she drives away, but Lila knows how this goes. Lila knows what it's like to have every intention of standing your ground with the person that broke your heart, only to wave white flags and soften with the right persuasion.

It's as if the safe and comfortable bubble surrounding them has popped, and Lila can't help but feel like everything has just changed.

## CHAPTER TWENTY-TWO

Lila's apartment feels so much colder than it did when she left it this morning. She woke up wrapped in a comfortable cocoon in bed with Emory, but now, coming home alone after a long shift, the air feels different.

Erin came all the way from Seattle to talk face to face with Emory. Sure, maybe it's a desperate attempt at an apology after she blew up their life together, but if romance books have taught Lila anything, it could be a grand gesture. Emory may think it's a display of her undying love, sending her back into Erin's arms and on the first flight back to Seattle. The thought alone makes Lila sick, her stomach twisting into a hard knot.

Lila is waist deep in a worst case scenario spiral when she finally hears a knock at the door. Part of her is relieved, knowing that Emory is on the other side of that door and not in the arms of a beautiful blonde woman. But then, the thought hits her. Emory might have just come back to break the news to her in person, that this was just a fling, and she's going back to where her heart actually lies.

Lila could keep going back and forth if she allowed herself too, but with her heart thumping out of her chest, she opens the door.

"Hey," Emory says in a tone that feels somber, yet relieved to see Lila at the same time. Emory wraps her arms around her and pulls Lila into a hug, Lila holding on as long as she possibly can.

"Come in," Lila finally says quietly. She pulls back from Emory, opening the door fully to welcome her inside. "Are you okay?"

Emory lets out a deep breath as she sits down on Lila's couch, her discomfort obvious as Lila watches her. "I'm so sorry Lila. I never thought she would just show up like that."

"Emory," Lila says as she sits next to her on the couch. "Don't apologize, please. I just want you to be okay."

Emory reaches over and grabs Lila's hand, squeezing tight as she looks into Lila's eyes.

"Well, what happened?" Lila asks tentatively. She doesn't want to push her, but Lila's heart needs to know. She can't last another moment in this painful uncertainty.

"Well, when I left Seattle, I didn't make a big fuss of it. I didn't want anyone to know, or for anyone to try to talk me out of it. I only told Becca once I got to Texas, but I asked her not to tell anyone, especially Erin and Avery."

Lila watches as Emory shakes her head, clearly realizing that she couldn't keep her cross country move a secret for long.

"I should have considered the fact that Becca can't keep a secret for the life of her, so Becca folded pretty quickly when Erin started asking questions."

"So...why did she come all the way here?" Lila asks, unsure if she even wants to hear the answer.

"She says that she always held out hope that we'd get back together, that we'd somehow be able to work through this and move forward. Apparently me leaving felt like the door was shutting on that happening, even though she failed to realize that I slammed the door on us a long time ago. She thought if she could just talk to me, that she could convince me to come back."

"Why would she come all the way here for that? She couldn't just call you like a normal person?"

Lila didn't mean to sound harsh, but the words flowed out of her mouth without control.

"Well, she did. Or she tried."

"What do you mean?" Lila asks, thinking back to their conversation last night.

"She did try to get in touch with me once she found out I left Seattle. She called me a few times, and she sent a long text apologizing for everything that happened between us, asking me to come back."

"Wait," Lila says as she processes it. "When did this happen?"

"About a week ago, maybe? It was the first night we got to Austin, actually."

"Austin?" Lila asks, her heart dropping into her stomach. She remembers waking up to the sound of Emory's phone buzzing on the nightstand, and how Emory immediately went cold when she looked at the phone screen. "Why didn't you tell me this?"

"What?" Emory asks. "It was before anything happened between us. We weren't where we're at now."

"Maybe not then, but what about last night? I asked you about what happened between you two, and you made it seem like the story ended when you moved out of your shared apartment."

"Because that is when it ended between her and I, Lila. There has been nothing since."

"But that's not true," Lila says. "You're telling me now that there's been texts and calls as recent as a week ago. You left that part of the story out."

Lila is immediately sent back into the past, to all the relationships filled with secrets and hidden contact. She remembers that painful pit in her stomach when she learned about Arthur entertaining other women, trying like hell to deny it or minimize her implications.

"Lila, I'm sorry," Emory says as she moves closer to Lila, squeezing her hand. "I didn't think it mattered. I never thought she would show up here!"

"It matters to me, Emory. When you leave out parts of the truth, it makes me question everything you said." As much as this moment hurts, Lila can't help but feel some comfort in the familiarity of it. Why would she think this thing with Emory was any different than what she's had before?

"Her reaching out to me didn't change anything about what I shared with you. When I saw her name on my screen that night, I blocked her immediately. I had no intention of letting her back into my world, and I still don't. Lila," Emory says, pausing to find the right words.

"I didn't mention her reaching out to me last week because I didn't want you to think there was anything there, anything recent. I meant it when I said I was done with her the moment I walked out of our home. Her apology and her desire to get me back to Seattle changes nothing for me. You are the only one I want."

Lila pulls her hand away from Emory, tucking it back into the safety of her lap. "No, hiding parts of the truth is still lying," Lila says, her stomach churning with every word. "This is no different than anything I've been involved with before."

Emory sits back as Lila says the words. "Hey, don't compare this to your cheating exes, Lila. You know this isn't the same."

"Well it feels the same," Lila snaps back, delivering her message as clearly as she can. They sit quietly, neither of them knowing how to repair this.

"Do you think I don't understand how much it hurts to be lied to? It's the reason I'm in this mess to begin with!" Emory snaps. "I wouldn't do that to you, Lila. That's not what this is."

Lila stares at the ground, unable to meet Emory's eyes. Her heart feels like it's cracking in two, a complete one-eighty to the warmth she felt in her chest just hours ago, before Emory's ex showed up and brought their journey to a screeching halt. Lila could have sworn that this thing with Emory was different, that they were two people coming together after being miserably broken.

Lila can feel her heart hardening with every passing second, and though it feels impossible, she finally says the words. "I want you to go."

Lila can hear Emory let out a quiet gasp, as if the words have knocked the air right out of her lungs.

"What?" Emory asks as she looks at Lila, silently pleading for her to look back. "You can't be serious?"

A few seconds pass, but Lila still says nothing, unable to meet Emory's eyes as she stands firm in her decision.

"Is that what you really want? For me to leave?" Emory asks as her voice shakes, as if she's on the verge of crumbling. Lila fights like hell to hold back her own sadness, but she knows she's moments away from breaking.

"Yes....please go," Lila answers quietly.

Emory remains seated at Lila's side, squeezing her hand one last time in an effort to get Lila to look at her, to change her mind. Lila doesn't budge.

Accepting their reality, Emory stands up from the couch, and she drags her feet to the door. The door closes behind her, and Lila finally allows herself to break. She sits in this feeling as the tears roll down her cheeks, a feeling she knows all too well.

## CHAPTER TWENTY-THREE

"Girl, we have to get you out of this apartment," Zoey says to Lila as she lays next to her in bed, the place where Lila has spent most of her time over the last three days. She hasn't talked to Emory since she walked out of her apartment, so hiding away from the world with Oliver is about all she can handle.

"Ugh," Lila says, "I don't feel like it Zoe."

"Duh! But once you get up and move, you'll feel better!" Zoey declares as she stands up from the bed, reaching over to tug on Lila's arm. "We don't have to do anything crazy. Let's just go have a drink at Patty's. We'll only be out for a couple hours."

A few moments pass, but Lila still hasn't budged. She tried to remain unconscious as much as possible over the last few days to ignore her current reality, but here it is, standing at the end of her bed and begging her to get up.

"Lila, you're going to be okay," Zoey says in a reassuring tone. "I know it hurts, but you're going to get through this. We're going to face this together."

"I know I will Zoey, but I'm just so tired of this. When will I ever get it right?" Lila asks, her voice starting to waiver.

"It's going to happen one day Lila, I promise you," Zoey

says. "And once it does, it will be worth all the shit you had to wade through to get there."

Zoey sits down on the bed and places her hand on Lila's. "Come on, let's get you up and moving. It'll help, I promise."

Lila lets out a huff, knowing Zoey will only keep trying to convince her if she doesn't give in.

"Alright, fine," Lila says as she climbs out of her bed. "I'm wearing this though, I'm not getting ready." Lila is wearing an oversized hoodie and sweatpants, her outfit looking just about as drab as Lila feels.

"Oh, as opposed to your standard red carpet fashion?" Zoey says with a laugh.

To show support for her best friend, Zoey raids Lila's closet, pulling out an outfit choice that matches Lila's current aesthetic. Zoey throws the hoodie over her tank top, and switches her jeans out for a pair of leggings. "Okay, now we match, let's go!"

∼

Thankfully, there doesn't appear to be any bachelorettes or divorcées at Patty's tonight. The main bar is filled with regulars, but at least that's a crowd that Lila can handle in her current state.

Lila and Zoey walk to the end of the bar to find two empty seats, when suddenly, Lila stops dead in her tracks. "You're kidding," Lila says with a straight face as she looks at Zoey.

"What?" Zoey says before she realizes what's wrong, but reality sets in once her eyes follow the direction Lila is pointing in.

Arthur.

"You're right, this is so much better than being in the comfort of my home," Lila says sarcastically to Zoey, trying to figure out if she should take this as a sign to make a swift exit.

"I'm sorry! I never see him here anymore. I didn't think

this was a possibility we had to worry about," Zoey says apologetically.

If she leaves now, Lila can probably sneak out of the building before Arthur even—

"Lila, Zoey. Hey," Arthur calls out once his gaze swings their way, only a handful of feet from where he's sitting.

"Heyyy," Lila says as she realizes her grand escape is no longer an option, and Arthur immediately picks up on her annoyance with his existence.

"Well, sorry for bringing down the vibe by being in your line of sight," Arthur says sarcastically.

"Nahh, she was already in a bad mood when she walked into the bar. You just made it worse," Zoey chimes in with a laugh.

"Ahh, well that makes me feel better," Arthur says as he nods his head.

With no other seating options available, Lila sits on the barstool next to Arthur, Zoey on the other side of her. Lila can feel beams of annoyance radiating off her skin, and it's clear that Arthur can sense it as well.

"Aside from my contribution to your mood," Arthur says with a smirk. "What's got you down?"

"I think you might be the last person she wants to talk to about this," Zoey comments.

"Actually," Lila says as she perks up, turning in her seat to face Arthur head on. "You're the perfect person to talk to about this."

"Oh?" Arthur says surprised.

"Oh yeah," Lila says. "Tell me, why do people lie? Why is it so hard for people to simply tell the truth? And not just bits and pieces of the truth, but the entire truth?"

"Uhhhhh...." Arthur says confused.

Zoey buries her head and laughs.

"No use in hiding it now," Lila says with a huff. "I was seeing Emory, or, I don't really know what we were doing. But we were doing something."

"I gathered," Arthur nods. "And something happened, I'm assuming?"

"Your assumptions would be correct."

"Oh," Arthur says, sounding shockingly saddened by the confession. "I'm sorry to hear that."

"Are you, though?" Lila asks sarcastically, thinking back to Arthur's outburst in the treatment area when Zoey asked about her boring date. Lila finds herself wishing she could go back in time to that dull evening, because as insufferable as it was, at least she wouldn't feel the way she does now.

"I am, actually. It seemed like she really liked you."

Lila cocks her head back at this response, wondering how Arthur would know anything about how Emory feels, or felt. "How would you know that?"

"Because she basically told me she did."

"Wait," Lila says shocked, racking her brain for how this could even be possible. "When could she have told you this?"

"During Bella's surgery."

Though Arthur seems happy to offer her crumbs and short sentences as an explanation, this will simply not do for Lila.

"Okay, start from the top," Lila says as she looks at Arthur, shocked by his response to all of this.

"Well, I may have been out of line to start with," Arthur answers. "But, I heard Zoey mention Emory to you, and then after seeing you two in the pharmacy together—it was pretty obvious."

"So...this is the part that was probably out of line on my part." Lila raises her eyebrows, waiting for him to spill it already. "I asked her if you two were seeing each other."

"Oh god," Lila answers, burying her face in her hands and imagining just how awkward that must have been for both of them, especially Emory. "And, what did she say?"

"She said yes."

"You are giving me the tiniest crumbs of information and

it's driving me insane," Lila says, and Arthur laughs at her frustration.

"Okay. When she said yes, I told her that I wish you two the best of luck. Her response to that was 'I don't need luck, because I'm not going to fuck it up the way you did.'"

Lila's cheeks burn at the thought of Emory not only saying these words out loud, but saying them so confidently to a man that actually did screw it all up. Royally.

"She got me on that one, so I laughed, of course—and the rest of the surgery was fine from there," Arthur says.

No matter how much this makes Lila's heart flutter, it doesn't change where they are now. Emory was already keeping things from her at this point, so what Arthur is telling her doesn't make a difference.

"Look, I don't know what happened between you two," Arthur says as he turns his head towards Lila again. "But maybe it's worth reconsidering. Despite what you may think, I do want you to be happy. And it really seemed like Emory wanted to be the one to make you happy."

Lila has been so mad at Arthur these last few months, she forgot just how kind he can actually be—when he wants to be at least. Lila meets his eyes again, letting her guard down and simply accepting the gesture he's offering.

"Well, thank you then," Lila responds, still mildly shocked that Arthur was encouraging her to be with anyone other than him. "I really do appreciate it."

"Anytime," Arthur nods, smiling over at Zoey as if this was a peace offering to her as well.

Usually, running into Arthur would have been the easiest way to ruin Lila's evening, especially in her current state. But to her surprise, and Zoey's, spending the evening with him wasn't awful. It may have actually been exactly what she needed.

## CHAPTER TWENTY-FOUR

Lila can't stop thinking about what Arthur said to her at Patty's. They called it an early night, just as Zoey said they would. But now, Lila is in her bed restless, tossing and turning as thoughts of Emory flood her mind.

Not only has her constant fidgeting prevented her from getting any sleep, but it's cutting into Oliver's restful slumber as well. Oliver insists on being glued to Lila the second she gets into bed, so her incessant tossing and turning has him glaring up at her in disgust.

It just doesn't make sense. If Emory was hell bent on doing things right with Lila, then how did they get here?

She thinks back to the last time she saw Emory, sitting on her couch and begging Lila to please understand, to just hear her out. She remembers the look in her eye as she asked Emory to leave, as if it's the very last thing Emory wanted to do.

Just a few weeks ago, before Emory crashed into her life, she asked Zoey why she always ends up right back where she started. Heart broken and alone, chasing after the next person that could never truly love her. But is that what this is? Is Emory just another emotionally unavailable partner that she can never truly have?

*And when you do manage to find something good with someone, you push them out of your life as quickly as they entered it.*

Is this what Lila was doing? Turning to her standard pattern of self destruction, pushing away anyone that may actually want to build something real with her? Her head spins at the thought.

*Is that what you really want? For me to leave?*

Her stomach drops as the memory of Emory saying this flashes in front of her eyes, her heart likely pleading with Lila to say anything other than 'yes, please go'. Telling Emory to leave seemed like the right decision at the time, one that would guard Lila's heart from shattering any more than it already had. But as Lila dives deeper into her thoughts, she wonders if maybe it was just the easiest option - one that would prevent her from having to explore a path entirely unknown to her. One that would require her to have faith in someone else, to trust someone else.

Emory pushed back at Lila's accusations, the ones that accused Emory of being just as deceitful as her exes. Even Lila knew at the time that it was an unfair comparison to make, but now, as she's remembering her final moments with Emory, she's beginning to think that her words were actually cruel. Emory had never given Lila a single reason to distrust her, but Lila pushed her out without a second thought, closing herself off to any explanation Emory could offer.

The realization slams into Lila with a dizzying force, her thoughts racing as she processes what this all means. She's the one that screwed this up. She pushed Emory away, the first person in a long time that may have actually wanted to build something real with Lila. Something meaningful. Something that could actually last.

Lila sits up in bed, suddenly consumed with hope that Emory has tried to reach out to her. Anticipation floods her mind as she reaches for her phone on the nightstand, but there's nothing. She hasn't called.

Realizing now that Lila is the one that should be doing all

the apologizing, she calls Emory herself, but nothing. No answer.

She can't stand the thought of lying in bed another moment, wondering where Emory is and what she is thinking. Is she okay? Is she sad? Is she falling apart the way Lila is right now? She springs out of bed in a fever, throwing on the hoodie and sweatpants she wore to Patty's.

She grabs her purse and her keys in a hurry, ready to drive over to Emory's place with her own grand gesture of an apology. She briefly considers what she can bring to Emory that falls somewhere in between flowers and cat grass, but there's no time for that.

Lila unlocks her door and flings it open, yelling behind her to say goodbye to Oliver. She bounds out of her apartment full steam ahead, when suddenly, she collides with something—or someone.

"Oh, god," Lila says as she holds her head, the hallway briefly spinning after the collision.

As the world settles and Lila can see what's in front of her, she sees Emory sitting on the floor beside her, her purse and its belongings scattered everywhere. The sight sends her back in time to an unexpected doorway collision just a few weeks ago, the moment when this beautiful stranger first crashed into her life.

"I'm sorry! I was just about to knock on your door when—"

Lila throws her arms around Emory's neck, practically tackling her as she dives in for a hug. Emory immediately wraps her arms around Lila's waist, pulling her in close until she's straddling Emory's lap. They hold each other as if they've been dying to, as if these last three days of uncertainty were torture for both of them.

"I'm so sorry Lila, I should have told you everything."

"No, please don't apologize, Emory. I'm the one that should be saying sorry. I was being ridiculous," Lila says as she leans back to look at Emory, brushing a fallen strand of hair behind her ear.

"I'm so sorry for asking you to leave. I should have just listened to you." Emory's arms are still wrapped around Lila's waist, holding on to her as if she never wants to let her go.

"You've never given me a reason to doubt you, or to doubt what this is—what this could be. I let all the shitty partners and the lies creep into what we have, and I messed everything up. I'm just so sorry. I want to give you and I a real shot," Lila says as she looks into Emory's hazel eyes. "I want that more than anything."

Lila has never been this vulnerable with anyone, but somehow, she knows her heart is safe here. Even if Emory decides this is too much, too complicated, telling Emory how she really feels will never be a mistake. "Do you still want this, with me?"

Lila was riding a high when she flew out of her apartment, determined to win Emory's heart back if it was the last thing she did. But now, as Emory sits glassy eyed and staring back at her, she no longer feels indestructible. Emory could say no, and though it would shatter her heart to pieces, she'd understand. Lila was the one that pushed Emory away after all, and she would have to find a way to be okay with that.

Lila studies Emory's face for any sign of an answer, seconds feeling like a lifetime as she waits for her reply. But just as Lila begins to lose hope, a smile spreads across Emory's face, and that perfect dimple of hers makes an appearance.

"Well then, lucky for you…there's nothing I want more."

Lila cups Emory's face in her hands, pulling her in until their lips crash together. They may have shared kisses before this moment, but somehow, this one feels like their first.

The first of many kisses as two people who came into each other's lives when they needed it most, committed to leaving everything else behind and choosing each other. Emory crashed into Lila's world when she least expected it, but now, she can't imagine a world without her.

# 1 YEAR LATER

"What if we forgot something?" Lila asks Emory, her lips practically quivering as she says the words.

"We didn't. We went over our checklist like twenty times," Emory answers with a laugh.

"Okay, well what if one of us has a medical emergency of some sort? What will we do?" Lila huffs.

"Well, that's what insurance is for. We'll be fine."

"But what about Oliver! He's going to be so confused—"

"Lila, it's going to be fine," Emory says as she places her hand on Lila's. "Oliver is happy with Zoey. We have everything we need. And neither of us are going to fall dead of a mysterious plague."

"I know, I know," Lila sighs as she squeezes Emory's hand. "I'm just nervous. I can't believe I'm actually doing this. I didn't make it this far before!"

Lila focuses on taking deep breaths, finally allowing her body to deflate and relax deeper into her seat. She leans her head against Emory's shoulder, feeling more thankful than ever for the incredible woman sitting next to her.

"I know you are, but I'll be here with you each step of the way." Emory leans over and places a kiss on Lila's cheek.

"Think of how incredible this will be, and we get to do it all with each other."

Emory's words send a wave of reassurance over her, and her trembling hands finally calm against Emory's touch.

"Think about it, in a few days, we'll be working alongside elephant vets and behaviorists. How many people get to do that?" Emory asks in Lila's ear.

*"Hello ladies and gentleman, welcome onboard flight KE 32 from Dallas, Texas to Seoul, Korea. We ask that you please fasten your seatbelts at this time, and secure all baggage underneath your seat or in the overhead compartments."*

Lila squeezes Emory's hand a bit tighter, trying to prepare herself for the voyage ahead.

"Try to close your eyes and get some rest," Emory says softly to Lila. "We'll be in Thailand before you know it."

# ACKNOWLEDGMENTS

First, I want to thank you for taking the time to read Heal My Fractious Heart. It's been a dream of mine to write a story that takes place in a veterinary setting, as well as one that highlights our work in the clinic. I hope you enjoyed reading it as much as I did writing it.

Special thanks to my friends that encouraged me to run with this idea, and those that allowed me to bounce ideas off of them. Your love and encouragement gave me the drive I needed to make this dream a reality. No matter how delusional my plotting and dreaming gets, you guys are there to hype me up each step of the way.

A big shout-out to my editor, Kristen, who helped me polish my manuscript into something I am proud of. I would be lost without your encouraging notes and skilled direction. I was actually put in touch with Kristen through my amazing cover designer, Lorissa. Lorissa brought my characters to life in a way I didn't think possible, and I will forever remember the moment I saw my characters in color for the first time.

And last, I want to thank my mom for the constant love and unwavering support she has shown me in each stage of my life. She sang a song to me when I was little that said "In all the world, you'll never find a love as true as mine," and it certainly rings true. Thank you for being my anchor in this stormy sea of life.

# ABOUT THE AUTHOR

Amber LaRock is the author of Heal My Fractious Heart, as well as a Licensed Veterinary Technician. She worked in emergency medicine for six years before transitioning into remote content creation for online pet brands, and eventually dove into the world of creative writing. She now lives in Chiang Mai, Thailand with her two cats, Oliver and Quinn.

Made in the USA
Columbia, SC
20 December 2024